The Testing of Tertius

Robert Newman

The Testing
of Tertius

Hutchinson of London

For Jessie and Ettore Rella

Hutchinson & Co (Publishers) Ltd
3 Fitzroy Square London W1

London Melbourne Sydney Auckland
Wellington Johannesburg Cape Town
and agencies throughout the world

First published in Great Britain 1974
© Robert Newman 1973

Set in Monotype Baskerville
Printed and bound in Great Britain by
R J Acford Ltd Industrial Estate
Chichester Sussex

ISBN   009 119460 1

To the reader:

Though this book is complete in itself and may be read by itself, it continues the adventures of characters introduced in MERLIN'S MISTAKE and therefore it might be useful to recount some of what happened in that earlier book.

On his sixteenth birthday Brian, only son of Sir Owaine of Caercorbin, met Tertius, a young page, in the forest and discovered that he was on a curious quest. Merlin, the great magician, had been Tertius' godfather and in attempting to endow him with all possible wisdom he had made a mistake. For the knowledge that he had absentmindedly bestowed on him was all *future* knowledge. Thus, while Tertius knew all about lasers, computers and nuclear reactors, he could not—as he said himself—cast a simple spell to cure warts. As a result he was trying to find a magician who could teach him magic that would be more appropriate to his time.

Brian decided to accompany Tertius on his quest and soon found one of his own. For when they arrived in Meliot they discovered that the town was being oppressed by the apparently invincible Black Knight and his men. Brian fought the Black Knight and was beaten and wounded. Nursed back to health by the Princess Lianor,

5

he fell in love with her twin sister, the Princess Alys, and determined that he would find the Knight with the Red Shield, who was said to be the only man who could conquer the Black Knight and free Meliot.

Accompanied by a strange old crone who called herself Maude, Brian and Tertius set out on their double quest. They were guided on the first stage of this by Brian's friend, the outlaw Long Hugh, and met the mysterious White Lady who told them cryptically how they would know the Knight with the Red Shield when they found him.

Shortly after that Brian's sword was stolen, and he replaced it with another which he found in an ancient burial mound and named Starflame. As their quest continued they made friends, with Migbeg, a Pictish chieftain, fought outlaws and had an encounter with a dragon and an unusual giant named Giles. Their quest finally took them to Cornwall where they were imprisoned by the Lady Nimue who had put Merlin under a spell. Using his anachronistic knowledge, Tertius freed Merlin. At the same time Brian discovered that he himself was the Knight with the Red Shield and also realized that the old crone Maude was really the Princess Lianor in disguise.

Returning to Meliot, Brian again fought the Black Knight and this time overcame him and there was a final revelation. For the Black Knight turned out to be his father who had supposedly been killed in the Crusades but who had lost his memory as a result of a head wound and did not know who he was until after his battle with Brian.

Tertius' quest ended as happily as Brian's for, recognizing his abilities, Merlin himself agreed to instruct him in magic.

I

If it is true that no one knows how things will end—and
they had to accept this since it was told to them by the
White Lady herself—it is also true that beginnings are
rarely recognized. But in this case they both knew it at
once. For no matter where or when it actually began, it
began for them that afternoon.

'Could it be the weather?' asked Brian. 'Because
there's a storm brewing?'

'Does it look as if we're going to have a storm?' asked
Lianor.

Brian looked up and around but except for a few high
clouds that moved slowly over the hills beyond Meliot
like grazing sheep the sky was clear and blue.

'No. Besides you say you've felt this way for some
time.'

'Yes.'

'How long?'

'Almost a week.'

He nodded. It had been about then that he had first
become aware of her strangeness and he had thought at
first that it was because of the wedding. For her twin
sister Alys was soon to be married while he and Lianor
had agreed to wait for at least another year, until Brian
was eighteen, before they were wed. And though Lianor

had denied that she cared about this he was not sure he believed her. That was one of the reasons he had suggested that they go hawking—to get her away from the palace where all the activity seemed to centre around Alys and the preparations for the wedding.

He had been wrong about that, it seemed. But coming out here into the fields had at least made her speak more openly about what was troubling her.

'And that's all you can tell me?' he said. 'That you've been feeling anxious.'

'I've been having dreams too, ones that I cannot remember.' Then, somewhat defensively, 'I've never dreamed lightly. Usually my dreams mean something.'

'And these?'

'How can I say what they mean when I don't remember them? All I am left with is a feeling of dread—a sense that somewhere not too far off—something is happening that threatens us all.'

Again Brian nodded. During the year or so that he had known her he had learned to respect these feelings of hers. For she had often known or sensed things that there was no reason for her to know.

The peregrine, standing hooded on his left hand, shifted her grip slightly and without thinking he stroked her breast feathers.

'Talking about it will not help,' said Lianor. 'See if she's ready to fly.'

'I'm sure she is,' said Brian.

He dismounted, tossing the reins over Gaillard's head, and the huge white charger moved off a few paces and began grazing.

Pulling the peregrine's jesses free of the leash and varvel and twisting the ends so they would not interfere with her flight, he unhooded her. Almost at once she roused.

Gripping his gauntlet even more tightly, she raised all her feathers, shook herself and then fanned her long, pointed wings.

This was an important sign. When they had gone to the mews to get her, Wellias, the king's falconer, had been unwilling to let them take her for she had been in moult. But while they were arguing with him—every falconer is convinced that only he truly understands his falcons and can fly them properly—she had roused for the first time. And so, still reluctantly and with many unnecessary instructions, Wellias had hooded her and handed her over.

Now, having roused again, she looked around with alert, dark eyes. Her name was Garym and she was a haggard or passage falcon who had been taken wild when more than two years old and been manned through many sleepless nights by Wellias.

'Sha-hou!' cried Brian, casting her off into the wind.

She was away at once, swinging around in wide circles to gain her pitch. Up and up she climbed with both Brian and Lianor watching her with held breath, for there are few things as beautiful as a gyring falcon.

Finally, when she was waiting on, soaring with outstretched wings so high above them that she looked no larger than a lark, Brian signalled the page who had ridden out with them and he loosed the hounds who set off for the hedge that bordered the field. But before they reached it—and long before they had flushed out any birds that might be hiding there—Lianor exclaimed and, looking up again, Brian saw that Garym was stooping. Wings almost closed and feet extended, she was diving down.

For a moment they could not tell what her quarry was. Then suddenly it appeared—a pigeon flying low

9

over the hedgerow to their right and toward them.

'Brian, call her off! The pigeon's hurt!'

Brian had seen it too; that the pigeon was flying, not merely low but heavily, uncertainly. He grimaced and groaned softly, for it is no easy matter to call off a stooping falcon. But he unwound the lure and began swinging it and whistling shrilly.

Garym checked, hesitated. And as she did a partridge, put up by the hounds, rose on the far side of the field and made off downwind. Again Garym checked, then turned slightly and came on once more, the wind whistling in her bells. She struck the partridge in midflight like a thunderbolt. There was a puff of feathers and the partridge fell like a stone.

As Brian ran across the field he looked back and saw that the pigeon, instead of flying on, had gone straight to Lianor and that she was holding it against her bosom and stroking and comforting it.

He reached the partridge which Garym was holding with her foot. He let her feed for a moment, then made in to her, taking her on his glove and hooding her again. He put the partridge in his bag, then with Garym on his fist, went back toward Lianor.

She was still holding the pigeon but there was an odd expression on her face.

'Is it much hurt?' asked Brian.

'No. More weary than hurt. But look' And she held something out to him; a small piece of parchment rolled so tightly that it was no thicker than a skewer. He unrolled it carefully for it had been scraped so thin that it was almost transparent and saw that it was covered with a strange kind of writing; all straight or slightly slanted lines.

'Where did you get it?' he asked.

'It was tied to the pigeon's leg.'

'A message of some sort. Can you read it?'

'No. It's Ogham, the writing that the Druids use. But turn it over.'

He did, and there was more of the strange writing. But above it, in letters that were small but still clear and legible was written: To Merlinus Ambrosius. Urgent!

'Merlin!'

'Yes.'

'Could it have anything to do with what we were talking about—this feeling you've had?'

'That I still have. It might.'

They looked at one another for a moment. Then, calling to the page and telling him to follow with the hounds, Brian swung up on to Gaillard and he and Lianor set off back to Meliot at a gallop.

2

The window of the solar overlooked the palace garden and through it they could hear the twang of a harp as Sir Uriel tuned it and then began singing a chanson to Alys. It was one they had not heard before and they listened to it while King Galleron examined the small roll of parchment, looking at both sides of it.

'You say it was tied to the pigeon's leg?'

'Yes, Sire,' said Brian.

'You know how a pigeon will always return to its cote,' said Lianor. 'Merlin must have given it to someone—a friend or agent—to use in time of need.'

'You need not explain,' said the king. 'I have heard of such things before. I take it neither of you can read the message.'

'No, father,' said Lianor. 'But it must be important. It says "urgent!" '

'I don't doubt that it is,' said the king. 'What did you do with the pigeon?'

'We gave it to Wellias,' said Brian. 'He said he would tend it for a few days and then release it.'

'And where is Merlin? Somewhere in Northumberland, is he not?'

'Yes, Sire,' said Brian. 'In his tower on the coast. He told me how to reach it.'

'Then you intend to take the message to him?'

'I thought I would,' said Brian. 'As you know, my good friend, Tertius, is with him and I would like to see him again.'

'It's a long journey to Northumberland,' said the king. 'It will take at least ten days and perhaps longer. Even if Wellias kept the pigeon for a week it would still get there before you would.'

'But it might not get there at all,' said Lianor. 'It might be attacked again by a falcon or a hawk and this time it might not escape.'

'You seem strangely anxious to have Brian go,' said the king, looking at her shrewdly. 'Won't you miss him?'

'No, father,' said Lianor. 'For I thought I would go with him.'

'So I suspected,' said the king. 'Why?'

'Because if he went without me I *would* miss him. And because I'd like to see Tertius and Merlin again myself.'

'And those are your only reasons?'

'Aren't they sufficient?'

Sir Uriel had finished the chanson and now, through the open window, they heard Alys laughing.

'Perhaps,' said the king, studying her. 'I'm not sure how your sister will feel about it. You know how she depends on you.'

'The only things she has ever depended on me for are things she does not want to do herself.'

'And what about me?' asked the king. 'It may be that I have asked too much of you these past few years. But ever since your mother died . . .'

'Please, father,' said Lianor. 'I trust you will always count on me. But if it's the wedding you're concerned about, the plans for that have all been made and we will be back long before it is to take place.'

The king continued looking at her as affectionately as she was looking at him and Brian knew that he was thinking what he himself had thought: that it was because of the wedding that Lianor wanted to get away. Finally he nodded.

'Very well,' he said. Then to Brian, 'When would you like to leave?'

'I think it should be as soon as possible,' said Brian. 'Tomorrow?'

Again the king nodded. 'I will speak to Sir Amory and have him select the men-at-arms who will ride with you.'

'Thank you, father,' said Lianor.

And so early the next morning they gathered in the courtyard: Brian, Lianor and ten men-at-arms, three of whom led sumpter mules carrying clothing and provisions. Brian held Gaillard by the reins while Lianor stood beside Gracielle, the yellow mare that had served her so well in the past. The king had come out to bid them farewell.

'When Sir Uriel arrived,' he said, 'he brought word that our liege, King Arthur, was on his way to France. It may be that the message concerns him. If it does and if either he or Merlin need me, let me know at once.'

'We will, Sire,' said Brian. 'As for the princess . . .'

'If I had any doubt that she was in good hands do you think I would let her go? But I will still not be easy until you are both home again. So go safely and return as quickly as you can.'

He embraced Brian, kissed Lianor and then they mounted and rode out of the courtyard, through the narrow streets to the town gates. From there they took the road to the ford, crossed it and started northeast through the forest towards Northumberland.

The king's guess as to the length of their journey had been a good one. Though they rode hard, starting at sunrise each morning, it took them ten days to reach the Humber. They crossed it on a ferry, a large, clumsy barge with four men at the sweeps, and then rode almost due north along the coast.

The weather had been settled, clear and sunny, ever since they left Meliot. But once they crossed the Humber the sky darkened and became heavy with clouds. They spent their first night in Northumberland in a manor house a few miles from the coast and when they left in the morning the bailiff told them they would have a wet ride for it was sure to rain before noon.

For a time it looked as if he were right. The clouds moved down from the north and became heavier and darker and a few raindrops fell. But when they paused for their midday meal the sky cleared directly overhead and they were able to eat in comfort. As they rode on, however, the clouds closed in once more and the sky became more threatening than ever.

'I wish it would make up its mind,' said Brian impatiently.

'It may be that the weather is like that here,' said Lianor. 'On the other hand, there may be another explanation for it.'

'What do you mean?' asked Brian.

'Tertius,' said Lianor. 'I don't know how long it takes to learn to control the weather, but he's only been studying with Merlin for about a year.'

'You're right,' said Brian, grinning. 'It could be Tertius.'

The weather continued to be uncertain as they rode up

the coast; the sky lowering threateningly, then clearing briefly. About the middle of the afternoon they saw a lonely tower on the edge of the cliffs that bordered the sea. As they approached it a single horseman came out of it and rode towards them; a rather small, slight, grey-haired man who looked dignified but by no means solemn.

'A very good day to you,' he said when he reached them. 'I am Stokely, Merlin's steward. I have come to welcome you in his name and in that of Master Tertius.'

'They knew we were coming?' asked Brian.

'They have known it for some time.'

'The pigeon,' guessed Lianor.

'She arrived here safely several days ago. With the message you left with your falconer. But Merlin did not need that. He has his own ways of knowing things.'

'I'm sure he has,' said Brian. Then as the steward turned his horse, escorting them back towards the tower, 'Is your weather here always so changeable?'

Stokely looked up at the dark clouds that were hanging over them again and smiled.

'No,' he said. 'Not when Merlin has it in hand. But of course Master Tertius is still learning.'

'That's what we thought,' said Lianor, smiling also.

There was a stone platform at the base of the tower with a parapet around it and steps leading up to it. As Lianor and Brian dismounted, Merlin and Tertius came out of the tower and stood at the top of the steps waiting for them.

Merlin was unchanged. His grey eyes were as keen as ever and with his long white beard, dark robe and small cap embroidered with cabalistic signs he looked as imposing as he always had. Tertius, however had grown in

16

the months since Brian and Lianor had last seen him and was both taller and thinner. And while he was still rather sober and serious he did not look quite so self-assured. In fact he seemed both awkward and uneasy. And since Merlin was frowning and pointedly ignoring him, the reason for it was fairly clear.

'Greetings, Merlin,' said Brian politely. 'It's been a long time. I trust you've been well?'

'Of course I've been well,' said Merlin testily. 'Why shouldn't I be?'

'All I meant was . . .'

'I know what you meant. All right, Tertius, Say hello to them and get it over with.'

'It's good to see you both again,' said Tertius.

'It's good to see you,' said Brian, wringing his hand.

'How was your journey?'

'Long, but not unpleasant,' said Lianor.

'And your father and sister?'

'Both well.'

'We bring you greetings from them,' said Brian to Merlin. 'Especially from the king.'

'I hope that's not all you've brought me.'

'You mean the message? Of course we brought that too. As we explained in our note, we were afraid to trust it to the pigeon again.'

'Yes, yes. Very sensible of you, though she got here safely. But I wish you had hurried. The message must be from my old friend and master, Blaise. I've been expecting it for weeks now and . . .'

The sky suddenly opened and the rain that had been threatening all day came down in torrents. Brian and Lianor quickly raised the hoods of their travelling cloaks but Merlin and Tertius merely stood there,

Tertius looking shocked and Merlin furious. They continued to stand there for a moment, the rain drenching them. Finally,

'You!' said Merlin, glaring at Tertius.

'I'm sorry, Merlin,' he said. 'I'm afraid I wasn't paying attention.'

'How much attention does it take? Or intelligence? Or knowledge?' Then, looking up, 'Stop!'

At once the rain stopped. Muttering something under his breath, Merlin waved his hand. The clouds parted and the sun came out, shining more brightly than it had since they had crossed the Humber. Glaring at Tertius again, Merlin went into the tower.

'Stokely!' they heard him call. 'Get me another robe!'

Brian and Lianor dropped their hoods, neither of them daring to look at the other.

'It's all right,' said Tertius. 'You can laugh if you want to.'

He sounded so woebegone that Brian lost all desire to.

'Don't you want to change also?' he asked.

'No,' said Tertius. 'But let's go inside. There's a fire there.'

They followed him in through the arched doorway and found themselves in a circular room that took up the whole of the first floor of the tower. There was a large fireplace opposite the doorway and near it were the stone stairs that led to the floors above. Brian and Lianor took off their cloaks and sat down on benches in front of the fire.

'It would seem that you've been having some trouble,' said Lianor to Tertius.

'Yes,' he said with a sigh. 'Especially lately. I don't have to tell you that Merlin's incredible. And while he's difficult at times, I've learned a great deal from him.

18

There are some things—things that have to do with people—that I can do well enough now to satisfy even him.'

'What do you mean by things that have to do with people?' asked Brian.

'Oh, making them do things or not do them. But there are other things that I've been having difficulties with.'

'Like the weather?' said Lianor.

'Yes. It's all very simple to Merlin. If you want to hold off a storm because you're concerned about your friends you just use the proper formula and that's it—you saw him just now. But even though I know it, while I'm saying it I'm thinking of weather patterns, isotherms and isobars, high and low pressure systems. And since I know that there's no scientific reason why the spell should work, very often it doesn't.'

'In other words, you know too much,' said Brian.

'Too much about the wrong things,' said Merlin coming down the stairs. 'I'm sometimes tempted to wipe all that nonsense out of his head and start him over again. But then I think that—even though it was my fault—perhaps what he knows has some purpose that even I'm not aware of yet. So I put up with it. And with him.'

'I said I was sorry,' said Tertius.

'I know, I know,' said Merlin. 'Now let me have that message.'

Brian took the small piece of parchment out of his pouch and gave it to him. Stepping closer to the fire, Merlin read it quickly. When he put it down again his face was grave.

'This is serious,' he said. 'More than serious.'

'Is it from Blaise?' asked Tertius.

'Yes. And it's about Urlik. Did you ever hear of

him?' he asked Brian and Lianor. 'Urlik the Black, sometimes called the Deathless?'

They shook their heads.

'We've known about him for a long time, Blaise and I,' said Merlin. 'It's one of the reasons Blaise took me as his pupil and taught me all he knew. And it's why I've been trying to do the same thing with Tertius.'

'Is he a magician too—this Urlik?' asked Brian.

'Not a magician, a wizard—a black wizard—and perhaps more than that. He could well be one of the Dark Powers or even the present manifestation of *the* Dark Power.'

'Is he here, in England?' asked Lianor.

'If he were you would have known it,' said Merlin grimly. 'Everyone would have known it save Blaise and me for we would have been the first he would have destroyed. No, we think he is still somewhere in the East. That is where he came from, the great plains beyond the Urals. Then, many years ago, he began moving westward with his hordes of horsemen. For a while the Russians held him at the Don. Then while I was—shall we say in seclusion?—there were reports that he had defeated the Russians and was moving again.'

'Reports from whom?' asked Brian.

'If there were only Blaise and I to oppose him the world would be in a parlous state,' said Merlin. 'For while his army is huge, savage and well-trained, Urlik himself is far more dangerous than it is. We had friends, white magicians like ourselves, in many parts of Europe who were just as concerned about him as we were. But one by one we stopped hearing from them. That is why Blaise himself went to France. For we both felt it was very important to learn what we could of Urlik's movements and, if possible, something about his plans.'

'And have you heard from him since?' asked Lianor.

'Yes, but not in several weeks,' said Merlin. 'This message says that Blaise now knows exactly what Urlik is up to and asks me to get in touch with him immediately.'

'And how will you do that?' asked Brian.

'You shall see,' said Merlin. 'This way.' And he led them up the stairs, past sleeping quarters and storerooms, to a room at the top of the tower. It was round like the one below, taking up the whole of the top of the tower. But unlike the lower room it was set about with windows so that there was no point in the wide horizon that could not been seen from it. There were many books in the room, old heavy volumes, most of them with clasps and locks on them. There was a table against one wall with curious instruments on it whose purpose Brian could not guess. And in the centre of the room was a stand with a large oval looking-glass on it.

Going to it, Merlin consulted the parchment Brian had given him and turned the mirror towards the southeast, for it was mounted on a pivot with a pointer set on a brass plate that gave the direction it was facing.

Adjusting the angle of the mirror carefully, Merlin stepped in front of it. He looked past it, out through the window which overlooked the high cliffs on which the tower stood, the sea pounding and roaring far below them. Then he whispered something under his breath, passing first his right and then his left hand over the glass.

The mirror had been cloudy at first, so cloudy that Merlin was reflected in it only dimly. But when he passed his hand over it his face vanished and another image appeared: that of a tower very much like the one they were in except that it was the keep of a formidable castle which stood, like Merlin's tower, on a cliff at the edge of the sea. This image was so sharp and clear that they could see the ivy on the grey stone walls. Then they seemed to move in through a narrow window to a room which again was very much like they were in and now, in the centre of the mirror, they saw the face of another elderly man, even older than Merlin.

He too wore a dark robe and a small round cap. And though his beard was longer and whiter than Merlin's the chief difference betweem then lay in their eyes. For while Merlin's were grey, sharp and penetrating, those of the man in the mirror were blue, lacklustre and even somewhat vacant.

'Blaise?' said Merlin.

The white-haired man was sitting in a chair, looking down. Now he slowly raised his head until he was looking directly at Merlin.

'Is anything wrong, Blaise?' asked Merlin. 'You look strange. As if . . .'

He broke off, for suddenly another figure appeared behind Blaise, then stepped in front of him so that his face filled the whole mirror—and it was a face that Brian knew he would never forget: a face such as we see only in nightmares.

This man's hair was black and cropped close. And though his beard was short and cut square, it was so thick that it did not seem to be a beard at all but rather a dark emanation—as if his body could not contain either his blackness or his strength. But what was most terrifying about him were his eyes: oblique, greenish and feral. They blazed out of the mirror like evil stars on a night of disaster.

He thrust out a hand at Merlin, two fingers forked like a snake's tongue, and Merlin staggered back, threw up his hands and fell to the floor as if he had been poleaxed.

3

For a moment they all stood there, frozen. Brian was so shocked and incredulous that he was not even conscious of the fear he had felt when he first saw that dark, bearded face. Then he turned back to the mirror. The face was still there and now the greenish eyes were on him. As his own eyes met them he felt himself gripped, held, and a strange weakness came over him as if something deep within him—something vital—was being drained out of him. His knees began to give way and he swayed—and as he did, Tertius moved. His face pale and set, he stepped in front of the mirror and passed first his left and then his right hand over it as Merlin had done. The dark face disappeared and the mirror became dim and cloudy again.

Lianor was beside Brian now, holding him up.

'Brian . . .'

'I'm all right,' he said, straightening up. 'What about Merlin?'

Lianor looked at him searchingly, then released him and all three of them bent over the elderly enchanter. He lay on his back, rigid, but with his eyes open, staring up at the low, beamed ceiling.

'There's a pallet over there,' said Tertius. 'Help me carry him over to it.'

They picked him up, carried him to the straw filled pallet near the wall and laid him gently down on it. Then Lianor knelt down beside him and put her ear to his chest while Tertius picked up one of his wrists, feeling for his pulse, and at the same time examined his eyes.

'Is he dead?' asked Brian.

'No,' said Lianor. 'His heart is still beating, but very weakly. I've never heard a heart beat so slowly.'

Tertius got to his feet, went to the door and called, 'Stokely!'

There were footsteps on the stairs and the grey-haired steward came into the room. His eyes widened when he saw Merlin lying on the pallet. He hurried to him, examined him and then looked at Tertius.

'It was Urlik,' said Tertius. 'The message from Blaise was a trap; Urlik already has him in his power. When Merlin tried to reach Blaise with the mirror, Urlik put a spell on him.'

'That's impossible!' said Stokely.

Brian knew how he felt. Merlin's wisdom and powers were legendary but they were also very real. For years he had been the king's adviser and as much Britain's guardian as the seas and cliffs that surrounded it. It was incredible that anything could happen to him; incredible and frightening.

'Can you break the spell?' asked Stokely.

'No,' said Tertius. 'At least not now.'

'Where is Urlik? Do you know?'

'Yes, I think so,' said Tertius. He went to the mirror and studied the pointer at its base that showed which way it was facing. 'He's in a castle somewhere on the coast of France, either in Brittany or Normandy.'

'That close?'

'Yes.'

'What's to be done?'

'If he's the threat that Merlin said he was,' said Brian, 'the king should be told at once.'

'Arthur's not here,' said Tertius. 'He's already in France.'

'Then he knew about Urlik?'

'No,' said Tertius. 'He went to help the Franks fight the Moors who are driving up from Spain. He took a hundred knights and several thousand men-at-arms with him. Merlin was uneasy about it and didn't want him to go, but he couldn't stop him.'

'That was probably part of Urlik's plot too,' said Stokely. 'To draw the king and his army away and leave Britain undefended.'

'Very likely.'

'Then that's all the more reason why he should be told,' said Brian.

'Yes,' said Tertius. 'He should be. But that's not enough. Arthur can't deal with Urlik.'

'Who can?'

'The only two who might be able to are Merlin and Blaise.'

'But they couldn't. You said yourself that Blaise was in his power and now he's struck down Merlin also.'

'That was because he was taken by surprise. I think, if he was prepared, he could stand against him.'

'But he's helpless now. And you say you can't break the spell that's on him.'

'That doesn't mean it can't be broken. If I knew more about it—exactly what kind of spell it is . . .'

'If!' said Brian impatiently. 'And how will you find that out? Will you ask Urlik?'

'Don't, Brian,' said Lianor.

'I'm sorry. It's just that I feel so helpless.'

'I know,' said Tertius. 'And no, I wouldn't ask Urlik. But the spell wasn't worked with that one gesture. It's a difficult and complicated one. And that means it was written down somewhere.'

'But where?'

'I may be able to show you.'

Stepping in front of the mirror, Tertius passed his hands over it as Merlin had done, saying something under his breath. It brightened, cleared and the room they had seen before appeared in it again. But this time it was empty and they could see that it was very much like the room they were in. There was a table with strange instruments on it and several shelves of books.

'There,' said Tertius pointing to a large and ancient book with locks and clasps that was on a stand near the table. 'It might very well be in that.'

'But how could you get to it and read it?' asked Lianor.

'I don't know. I would have to find the castle first and then see.'

'Then you're going to France?' said Brian.

'Yes.'

'Alone?'

'I'd rather not go alone.'

'Ah,' said Brian, relieved. 'Then the two of us will go. Any others?'

'It might be helpful to take some others with us. Not too many for we'll be going to enemy country and have to move carefully, secretly.'

'There's no one better at that than Long Hugh.'

'That's what I thought—he and say two of his men. And perhaps Giles the Giant. He claims he hates violence, but I hope we will not have to do any fighting. If we do, he will be worth having along.'

'Since you seem to be thinking of old friends what about Migbeg?' asked Lianor. 'He is as good a tracker and stalker as Long Hugh and his outlaws.'

'He might be useful too,' agreed Tertius. 'But that would be about all. We would take Merlin with us.'

'How can we take him?'

'I think we can manage somehow.'

'But why do you want him with us?'

'So that if I can break the spell he can do whatever must be done to deal with Urlik at once.'

'Then I will come too,' said Stokely. 'He will need someone to tend him.'

'It would be better if you stayed here,' said Tertius. 'If we fail, as we may, we can't let the tower and all it contains fall into Urlik's hands. Someone completely trustworthy should be here to destroy it.'

'If you fail it will not matter what happens to the tower,' said Stokely. 'Merlin has been my master for many years and where he goes, I go.'

'Very well,' said Tertius. 'That is your right.'

'Now can we get to the expedition itself?' said Brian. 'I gather we must move fast. How are we to let Long Hugh and the others know that we need them?'

'With the mirror,' said Tertius. 'I'll take care of that. What else?'

'We'll need a ship to get to France.'

'Master Trask,' said Stokely.

'That was my thought,' said Tertius.

'Who's Master Trask?' asked Lianor.

'A shipmaster for whom Merlin has done many favours. He was here to see him only yesterday. We will ask him to sail us to one of the Cinque Ports—Sandwich might be best—and have the others meet us there. Stokely, will you go and see him and arrange it?'

'Of course. How many will we be in all?'

'There are the three of us,' said Tertius. 'Long Hugh and two of his men, Giles and Migbeg. Eight in all.'

'Nine,' said Lianor.

'Why nine?'

'Why do you think? I was in at the beginning of this and I intend to be in at the end.'

'That's ridiculous!' said Brian. 'This is no mission for a woman!'

'I was with you on your quest for the Knight with the Red Shield.'

'That was different. I did not know who you were then. I thought you were an old crone. And even then I would not have let you come if you had not tricked me into it.'

'Were you sorry I came?'

'No. But as I said, this is different.'

'The only way in which it is different is that it is much more important.'

'And much more dangerous. I promised your father I would look after you.'

'And how will you do that if you are in France?'

'But I will not need to if you go back to Meliot!'

'Brian, be reasonable. I was a great help to you on the quest. Tertius knew I would be even before we started out. I would be a help to you in this too.'

'I said this is no mission for a woman! You saw Urlik in the mirror and you must have some idea of what he's capable of! You will go back to Meliot in the morning!'

They glared at one another and Stokely hesitated, then looked at Tertius.

'Tell Master Trask that we'll be eight,' said Tertius. 'And Merlin.'

Stokely nodded and left.

'Now I'd better let our friends know,' said Tertius.

Unrolling a large map of Britain, he studied it for a minute, then turned the mirror to the southwest. He passed his hands over it, saying something under his breath, and it brightened, cleared and they were looking at a forest glade. A fire burned in its centre and lounging about it were a half dozen men in deerskin jerkins. Tertius adjusted the angle of the mirror slightly and now they could see Long Hugh sitting crosslegged in a hut on the far side of the glade and waxing a bowstring. Tertius stared at him fixedly and Long Hugh started and sat up as if someone had called him. He looked this way and that, finally looking directly at Tertius.

'Can he see us?' asked Brian.

'No,' said Tertius. 'Quiet.' He went on staring at Long Hugh, and the outlaw, looking first uneasy and then puzzled, remained still as if he were listening. Finally, shrugging, he got up. Walking to the fire, he called two of his men to him and began talking to them.

'All right,' said Tertius. 'He was a little difficult, but I think I got through to him. He will meet us in Sandwich in five days. Now for Migbeg.'

He turned the mirror slightly to the east and now they could see the heath in it; the barren wasteland where they had first met the Pictish chieftain. Again Tertius adjusted the mirror's angle until they saw Migbeg lying on a pile of furs in what seemed to be a cave and talking to a slim woman who was as dark-haired, strange and wild-looking as he was. Though he too looked startled at first, it seemed easier for Tertius to get his message to him than it had been to Long Hugh. After only a moment or two he got up also, slipped the sword Brian had given him through his belt, picked up his flint-headed spear and, after saying something to the woman, left the cave.

When Tertius got Giles in the mirror he was asleep in the huge chair near the fireplace of his cottage while his sister, Lamorna, stirred a pot that hung there on a crane. He must have taken the message to be a dream for, when he woke with a start and talked to Lamorna, she looked interested, but only nodded and smiled. As a result, Tertius apparently had to go through the whole thing again before Giles got up, picked up his club and prepared to leave the cottage.

Tertius passed his hands over the mirror again, making the cottage disappear, and then sat down with a tired sigh.

'Tertius,' said Lianor, 'are you sure you can do this?'

'Do what?'

'Everything. Lead the expedition to France, break the spell . . .'

'I don't know. But whatever I do, I won't be doing it alone. Brian will be with me.'

'I'll do what I can,' said Brian. 'But the responsibility will be mostly yours.'

'I know,' said Tertius. 'And I wish it weren't. But since there's no one else I must do what I can too.'

It was beginning to get dark now and when Stokely returned a short while later he brought a pair of candles with him. He went directly to Merlin and stood there looking down at him.

'No change?' he asked.

'No change,' said Tertius. 'And there won't be one until the spell is broken.'

'What about food and drink?'

'He will not need any,' said Tertius. 'He can stay this way for weeks, months, perhaps even longer. What about Trask?'

'He will take us wherever we want to go. We are to be at the harbour at dawn.'

'Then I think we should eat and get some rest for we will have to be up early.'

Stokely nodded. He was still standing there, looking down unhappily at Merlin's expressionless face and again Brian knew how he felt. It was not just incredible that Merlin should have been struck down this way, the victim of a spell, there was something very sad about it too.

'Even though he knows and feels nothing,' said Stokely. 'I would be happier if he spent this night at least in his own bed. Will you help me carry him there?'

'Of course,' said Tertius. And he and Brian helped him carry the enchanter down the stairs to a room on the floor below.

Supper was a silent meal. Though there was some talk about what they would need in the way of provisions for their expedition, Lianor did not take part in it. She had said nothing to Brian since their argument and said nothing to him while they ate, though he did see her talking earnestly to Stokely later on just before they all went up to their rooms.

The clink of arms and the sound of horses' hoofs woke Brian. He got up sleepily, went to the window of his room and looked out. It was still dark for it was well before dawn. But a stable boy stood at the foot of the steps holding a torch and by its light he could see the men-at-arms that King Galleron had sent with them waiting outside the tower. As he watched, Lianor came out wrapped in her travelling cloak. She mounted Gracielle, waved to someone in the doorway of the tower and rode off into the darkness followed by the men-at-arms.

Dressing quickly, Brian hurried down to the room below. Tertius and Stokely were both there, standing in front of the fireplace.

'Did I see the Princess Lianor leaving?' he asked Stokely.

'Yes, Sir Brian,' said the steward.

'Did she give you any message for me?'

'No, Sir Brian.'

Brian nodded as if he was not surprised, but he was both hurt and upset. And though he tried not to show it, it was clear from the way Tertius looked at him that he knew how he felt.

After they had broken their fast they went out also. Merlin, as still and rigid as he had been before, had been wrapped in blankets and lay on a litter that was slung between two horses, one in front and one behind.

Gaillard, happy to see Brian, nuzzled him as he checked his saddle girth. Brian patted him and mounted. A thick fog was rolling in from the sea and Stokely, riding a brown hackney, raised the hood of his cloak. The stable boy gave him the reins of the lead horse of the two that carried Merlin's litter and he rode off into the fog, followed by Brian and Tertius.

They rode across the headland on which the tower stood and down a path on the far side to a small harbour that was sheltered from the sullen grey waves of the North Sea by a breakwater. A broad-beamed, deep-bellied ship some sixty feet long was moored there. Its gangplank was out and standing on the quay and holding a lantern was a heavy-set, grey-bearded man wearing sea-boots and a woollen stocking cap.

'Greetings, Master Trask,' said Tertius.

'A good day to you, Master Tertius,' said the captain. He raised the lantern, looking down at Merlin. 'Though

I should not say that, for this is as bad and black a day as I have ever seen.'

'It is that,' said Tertius. 'This is my friend, Sir Brian of Caercorbin.'

Brian and Trask nodded to one another.

'Do you have a safe, warm place for Merlin?' asked Stokely. 'I would see him bestowed before we board oursleves.'

'He shall have my cabin,' said Trask. Calling two of his men, he had them unstrap the litter and carry it into a cabin in the sterncastle.

Standing on the cobbles of the quay, Brian looked at the beamy, blunt-nosed ship with its high forecastle and sterncastle. The name on her transom was *The Swallow of Whitby*. And though he knew nothing about ships or the sea, it seemed to him that he had never seen anything more unlike a swallow.

Master Trask, returning to the quay, saw the expression on his face and misread it.

'Nay, Sir Brian,' he said. 'Look not so uncertain. She is as well-found a cog as you will find on the entire coast. She will take you safely, not only to France, but much further if need be.'

'I'm sure she will,' said Brian. 'Shall we board now?'

'Aye,' said Trask. 'The horses first.'

Again he called to his men and two of them took the horses that had carried Merlin's litter and tried to lead them aboard. But, made nervous by the motion of the ship and the slow rise and fall of the gangplank, they reared, neighed and backed away.

'Wait,' said Brian. 'Let me take Gaillard aboard. They will follow him.'

Leading the charger to the head of the gangplank he talked to him soothingly for a moment. Gaillard snorted, tossing his head, then walked behind Brian across the swaying gangplank and down the incline into the ship's open hold.

Brian tied him to an iron ring, then turned. As he had thought, where Gaillard went the others followed, and in a few moments all the horses were aboard and safely tethered.

In the meantime, Master Trask had taken his place at the tiller. Tertius was standing near him and climbing the ladder that led up to the sterncastle, Brian joined them.

'All secure below?' called Trask.

'Aye, aye, sir,' answered one of the sailors.

The captain began giving his orders. The lines fore and aft were let go and hauled in. Two seamen swarmed up the backstays as nimbly as squirrels and unloosed the lashings of the large square sail, letting it drop and making it fast. Though the fog was still thick, a gentle but steady northeast wind was blowing. The sail filled and bellied and the ship moved away from the quay and out towards the breakwater.

Brian look back. The houses of the port were disappearing in the fog and his mood was as heavy and grey as the weather: not because of the difficulty of the task they faced and its dangers, but for reasons he would not have confessed to anyone. This was the first time that he and Lianor had been separated since they met and while he knew that she was angry at him, he still could not accept the fact that she had gone off without a word to him.

The *Swallow* sailed out through the opening in the breakwater and Trask set her course south. When she was clear of the headland, the wind freshened and she began pitching slightly to the send of the sea.

34

'I'm not sure how the horses will like this,' said Brian. 'Perhaps I'd better look at them.'

'Perhaps you should,' said Tertius.

Brian went down the ladder again into the open hold. He had not seen Stokely since they boarded the ship, but he caught a glimpse of him now. He was at the far end of the line of horses, his hood pulled forward and his cloak wrapped closely about him against the chill and the damp. Brian loosed Gaillard's girth, took off his saddle and laid it on the planking of the hold. He did the same thing for Tertius' grey palfrey. The two horses that had carried Merlin's litter did not seem too uneasy and Brian glanced past them, then stiffened. The last horse in the line was not Stokely's brown hackney, but Gracielle.

'What are you doing with the princess's horse?' he asked angrily.

The cloaked figure turned. It was not Stokely. It was Lianor.

4

'For once,' said Lianor, 'let's try and avoid the obvious. Don't ask me what I'm doing here.'

'You think that's obvious?'

'It should be. You know very well why I'm here.'

'I told you it was no mission for a woman!'

'I agree. And I'm not going as a woman. I'm going as your squire.' She threw back her hood and opened her cloak and he stared. She had cut her hair so that it was now no longer than his and, instead of a riding dress, she was wearing low boots, hose and a tunic.

'Do you think that will fool anyone?'

'Don't you?'

As a matter of fact, if one did not look at her too closely she could now pass as a rather slim youth, but Brian was not going to admit that.

'That has nothing to do with it. You know why I didn't want you to come with us.'

'Because it may be dangerous.'

'It's certain to be!'

'There's a good chance that it may be,' said Tertius, coming up behind them. 'But I wouldn't say it was certain.'

Brian turned. 'You knew about it, didn't you?'

'Yes.'

'Why did you let her do it?'

'You talk as if I could have stopped her.'

'You could have tried!'

Tertius shook his head. 'Once she had persuaded Stokely to lend her some clothes and let her go in his place, I knew it was useless.'

'I still think you could have tried,' said Brian. Then, 'How was she able to persuade Stokely to let her go in his place?'

'By pointing out to him what I did; that the tower was his responsibility. And by promising to take as good care of Merlin as he would himself.'

'But what about the danger? You know what we may be facing.'

'If we fail, Brian—if Urlik takes England—she would be no safer there than in France.'

'I suppose that's so,' said Brian. 'But I still don't like it.'

'There's little for any of us to like about it,' said Lianor. 'I asked you to be reasonable yesterday. Now I ask you to have faith.'

'In what?'

'In me, among other things. I told you that I was in at the beginning of this and that I intended to be in at the end. Well, I have a feeling . . . No, it's more than a feeling. I know I was meant to go with you.'

This of course was unanswerable.

'If that's true,' said Brian, 'what can I say?'

'Then there'll be no more arguing about it? You won't try and make me go home when we get to Sandwich?'

'No.'

'Good. Besides,' and she smiled, 'can you imagine what Alys would say if I went back to Meliot with my hair like this?'

The wind held steady for two days and at first it looked as if they would be early for their rendezvous. But on the third day it died and they spent several anxious hours rolling and pitching between the chalk cliffs and the sands offshore. However at dusk the wind came up again, still blowing from the northeast, and so on the morning of the fourth day of their voyage—the fifth since Tertius had sent his message—they put into the harbour at Sandwich.

It was a large harbour, filled with shipping, and Brian, Lianor and Tertius stood with Trask as he steered the *Swallow* between the craft at anchor and towards the quays.

'Where are you to meet your friends?' he asked.

'I did not say,' said Tertius. 'But we should have no trouble finding them.'

'You think not?'

'No.' Then pointing to a quay off to their right. 'There.'

Trask looked, blinked, and looked again. A small crowd had gathered on the quay and all those in it— seamen, watermen and porters—were jabbering, pointing and staring up at Giles. For though not quite as large as Gogmagog was said to have been, he was close to twelve feet tall.

'You did not tell me who or what he was,' said Trask somewhat reproachfully.

'Does it matter?' asked Lianor.

'I suppose not. And I probably should not be surprised since Merlin's friends are not often ordinary.'

He called to his men and two of them climbed the backstays and began furling the sail. As the *Swallow* drew closer to the quay Brian saw the others: Long Hugh leaning on his bow with Hob and Wat beside him and

Migbeg sitting on the edge of the quay with his bare legs dangling. He did not have blue paint on his face as he often did, but with his long black hair, bronze bracelets and flint-headed spear he looked strange enough. It was he who saw them first. Leaping to his feet, he tapped Long Hugh on the arm and gestured. Long Hugh, who had been scowling at the crowd, turned and when he saw them his face cleared. He waved and they waved back to him.

Trask put the *Swallow* neatly alongside the quay and his men made her fast.

'Shall we come aboard?' called Long Hugh.

'There is something I must do before we sail again,' said Trask, 'but you might as well.'

Hugh led the others aboard and Brian, Lianor and Tertius went down to the open hold to greet them.

'Well, Brian,' said Hugh, gripping his hand. 'I suppose I should say Sir Brian—and princess and Tertius—it's good to see you all again.'

'And good to get away from that crowd,' said Giles. 'I cannot say much for the manners of the folk in these parts. The way they've been staring you'd think they'd never seen a giant before.'

'Perhaps it was not you they were staring at,' said Lianor gravely. 'Perhaps it was Migbeg.'

Migbeg, who would not speak any language but his own though he understood everything that was said to him, smiled at this.

'Now perhaps you'll tell us what's afoot,' said Hugh. 'I thought I'd been moonstruck when I got your message. And so did Hob and Wat.'

'That we did,' said Wat. 'He comes out of his hut looking queer-like and says, "I'm off to Sandwich and you and Hob are coming with me." "Why?" I asks.

"I don't know" he says, "but I just got a message we should go there." "What kind of a message?" I asks. "From who?" "From Tertius," he says shortlike. "Now stop asking questions and let's be off." '

'I thought I'd dreamed it,' said Giles. 'I woke up and told Lamorna about it and she said maybe it wasn't a dream—she's clever about these things, you know. And then it came again—you, Tertius, saying I was to meet you here in five days.'

'You knew it was me?' asked Tertius.

'Yes,' said Giles. 'I don't know how, but I did.'

'We thought old Hugh had finally lost his wits,' said Hob. 'He wouldn't tell us how he'd gotten the message and he growled at us every time we asked him. We kept wondering what we should do about him—whether a blood-letting would help him—until we got here and found Giles and Migbeg.'

'I met Migbeg just outside of town,' said Giles, 'and we came here together. But as soon as I saw him I knew Lamorna was right and it was a true message.'

'Does it have something to do with Merlin?' asked Hugh.

'Yes,' said Tertius. 'And with England and many other things.'

'What other things?' asked Giles. 'And where is Merlin?'

'In the shipmaster's cabin,' said Tertius. 'Perhaps you'd better look at him and then we'll tell you what happened and what must be done about it.'

He led them to Trask's cabin and opened the door. The three outlaws, Giles and Migbeg looked in at Merlin who was lying rigid and with open and unseeing eyes in the shipmaster's bunk.

'Is he asleep?' asked Giles, stooping down so he could peer in.

'No, his eyes are open,' said Hugh. 'He must be sick. Or is it some kind of a spell?'

Migbeg shook his head. He tapped his chest and looked at Lianor who always understood his sign language better than anyone else.

'Hs heart?' she asked. Again Migbeg shook his head. 'His soul?'

Migbeg nodded, brought his hand up to his mouth, grasped something and drew it away.

'He says his soul has been stolen,' said Lianor.

'That's as good a way of putting it as any other,' said Tertius. 'Or you could call it a spell if you like.'

'But who did it?' asked Hugh. 'How? And why?'

'It's a strange, dark tale,' said Tertius, closing the cabin door, 'and a frightening one. Come up on to the sterncastle and I'll tell it to you.'

And when they were all disposed there he told them, not just about Urlik and what had happened, but what might happen and what they hoped to do about it. There was silence when he finished.

'You want us to come with you?' asked Hugh.

'We hoped you would,' said Brian.

'You are going, princess?' Hugh asked Lianor.

'Yes, Hugh.'

'From the way you're dressed, I thought so.' He considered for a moment. 'Wat and Hob must answer for themselves. As for me, I have long wished to see France. I will come.'

Hob and Wat exchanged glances. 'I don't know why you should want to see France,' said Hob. 'I don't hold with foreigners or foreign places. And I don't like the sound of this Urlik. But if I can help keep him away from here, I'll come too.'

'Foreigners don't bother me,' said Wat. 'My wife has Welsh cousins. It's the sea I don't like. From what I hear it can be dangerous. But if Hugh and Hob are going, I will go too.'

'Good,' said Tertius. 'Giles?'

'I hope it will not mean fighting,' he said. 'You know how I feel about violence. But if it is for Merlin and England, of course I'll come.'

'Did you understand everything that was said, Migbeg?' asked Lianor. And when he nodded, 'What say you? Will you come too?'

He gripped his left arm with his right hand and, frowning, shook it off. Then, tapping his chest and pointing to the east, he raised his spear menacingly.

'I think he means that his people have always fought with anyone who interfered with them,' said Lianor. 'And if that is what Urlik intends to do, of course he'll come with us.' And when he nodded again, 'Well, we seem to have our company.'

'Do you have any baggage?' asked Brian.

'Just this,' said Giles, holding up a leather sack that he had been carrying slung over his club.

'All we brought was some extra arrows,' said Hugh, gesturing towards two bundles of clothyard shafts that Hob and Wat had brought aboard. 'We thought it might be well to have them.'

'It may indeed,' said Trask who had been ashore and had now joined them. 'Three bowmen are better than none, but I wish we had a full company of them.'

'You have news?' Brian asked him.

'Yes', said Trask. 'I have been talking to shipmasters

who have been to France and the Low Countries recently and they have seen some strange and unlikely ships along the coast.'

'What sort of ships?' asked Tertius.

'Galleys from the far south,' said Trask. 'They would have the heels of us unless we had the right kind of wind and a long lead.'

'Then we shall have to try and avoid them,' said Brian.

'That we shall do if we can,' said Trask. 'But while it is good to be forewarned, it helps little to worry before there is need. Are you ready to sail?'

'We are,' said Tertius.

'Then we shall go now while the wind and tide serve.'

And taking the tiller, he began calling his orders. The hawsers were hauled in, the sail unfurled and the *Swallow* moved slowly away from the quay and towards the breakwater.

Lianor, Brian and Tertius walked to the rail and stood looking back at the town and the green countryside behind it.

'I wonder when we will see it again,' said Brian.

'I wonder *what* we will see when we see it again,' said Lianor.

'It will be the same,' said Brian. 'That is why we are going—to keep it the same.'

'How comforting it is,' said Tertius dryly, 'to be with an optimist again,' and he left them to talk to Trask.

The wind was from the north now and as the *Swallow* went out through the breakwater and began pitching in the following sea, Wat lost his colour and began looking as if his worst fears had been realized.

'Take him below,' said Trask. 'He will feel the motion less there.'

Hugh and Hob, who seemed in little better case than Wat, took him by the arms and helped him to the ladder.

'What does he mean by below?' asked Wat.

'I think the cabin,' said Hugh. 'Where Merlin is.'

'Oh, no,' groaned Wat. 'I made one mistake when I said I'd come on this devilish craft. I'm not going to make another. When I die, let it at least be in the open.'

And stretching out on a pile of hay near the horses, he closed his eyes, waiting for what he clearly hoped would be a speedy end.

5

For two days the weather remained fair and clear and they sailed south and west, keeping well away from the French coast. They saw no other ships during this time though Trask had ordered his men to keep a sharp lookout for them. On the morning of the third day, after consulting with Tertius, Trask changed course so that the *Swallow* was sailing almost due east.

'Where are we now?' asked Brian.

'If my reckoning is correct we should be off Little Britain that those in these parts call Armorica.'

'Shall we see it soon?' asked Lianor.

'I fear that before long we shall not be seeing anything.'

'Why do you say that?'

Trask jerked his head and, looking astern, Brian and Lianor saw a thick bank of fog moving toward them on the wind which was now westerly.

'You must have sailed in fog before,' said Brian, noting his frown.

'In waters I know,' said Trask. 'I don't know these. And when we get closer to land they become dangerous.'

'Should we hold off till the weather clears?' asked Tertius.

'No. You're anxious to get where you're going and

I'm anxious to get you there and be off again. Let's chance it.'

But he ordered men forward to the bow and up to the masthead, telling them to keep a sharper watch than ever.

A short while later the fog reached them and rolled over them and they sailed on in a wet, grey world in which they could barely see the bow from the sterncastle. They sailed thus for most of the morning, seeing nothing and hearing little but the slap of the waves and the creak of the rigging. Then, at about noon, there was a sudden cry of 'Breakers ahead,' from the bow.

'Where away?' shouted Trask.

'I can't see them. I can only hear them. I think off the port bow.'

'Keep watching and listening,' ordered Trask, bearing down on the tiller. As the *Swallow* swung to the starboard, Brian could hear it too; the sullen roar of waves breaking.

'Is it the coast?' asked Tertius.

'No. We're still too far out,' said Trask. 'It must be a rock or a reef.'

'Fog clearing ahead,' called the man at the masthead.

'Ah,' said Trask. 'Saint George is still with us.' Then, 'Maybe not. Listen!'

And now, along with the sound of the breakers, they could hear something else; a slow, rhythmic noise off to the starboard.

'It sounds like a drum,' said Brian.

'I fear it is,' said Trask, looking more grim than ever.

The fog was thinning now and they began to see patches of sea. Then suddenly they were out of the fog and there, a half mile or so away, was a long, low, many-oared ship as menacing as a shark.

'Well,' said Trask, 'the shipmasters at Sandwich were right. Foes are gathering from far and near.'

'What is she?' asked Brian.

'Saracen, I think,' said Trask. 'Yes, she's flying the Crescent.' Then, as the galley turned sharply towards them and the drum that gave the oarsmen their stroke began to beat more quickly, 'They've seen us.'

'Do we fight?' asked Hugh who had joined them.

'How can we? She must have over a hundred fighting men aboard her.'

'Do we run then?' asked Brian.

'We can't do that either. She's much too fast for us.'

Even those of them who were not seamen could see that this was true. For now the galley was driving toward them far more quickly than the *Swallow* had ever sailed even in half a gale, lifting with each stroke of its many oars and throwing up a white bow wave.

'Is there nothing that can be done then?'

'Yes,' said Trask. 'This.' And pushing the tiller over, he turned the *Swallow* back into the fog bank.

'What about the rocks?' asked Tertius.

'We'll have to risk them,' said Trask. 'There's no hope for us out in the open. But if any of you have specially sharp eyes you might go up to the bow.'

'I think I'll stay here,' said Hugh. 'I might be useful.'

'Migbeg!' called Lianor. Migbeg, who had been squatting in the hold with Hob and Wat, nodded, climbed the ladder to the forecastle and joined the seamen who were already there.

'Can't you do anything to help, Tertius?' asked Lianor.

'Like what?'

'Clear off the fog so we can see what's ahead of us.'

'You know how I am about weather, but I'll try.'

He turned so he was facing into the wind and raised his hands, saying something under his breath. Nothing happened. He repeated the gesture and the wind freshened a little, blowing more strongly and thinning out the fog ahead of them so that they could see perhaps a hundred yards. It remained as thick as ever behind them, however, and they could hear the drum on the galley as she hunted for them in the murk.

'Breakers ahead!' called the seaman in the bow for the second time.

'Can you see aught?' shouted Trask.

'No,' answered the seaman. Then, 'Yes! Hard aport!'

They saw it at almost the same time that he did; not a reef but a huge rock that loomed up higher than the mast. Trask pushed the tiller over again, keeping his eye on the sail that was starting to flap as it spilled the wind.

'We can't hold this course for long,' said Trask. 'Tell me when we've cleared it.'

They could see his dilemma. He could not bear farther to port without losing the wind. If they did that they would be swept broadside against the rock. But the course they were on was bringing them closer to the rock—and they were already so near that they could see the nests of the seabirds on its steep sides.

'It goes on and on,' called the seaman. 'I'm afraid . . .'

He broke off as Migbeg whistled shrilly, pointing somewhat to the starboard.

'What do you see?' asked the seaman impatiently. 'I see nothing.' Then, 'He's right. There's an opening.'

'Wide enough?' called Trask.

'With Saint Michael's help, it might be.'

Now they could see it too; a narrow opening between

the rock and another one that stood next to it. Brian studied the passage which seemed scarcely wider than the *Swallow*.

'It will be like threading a needle,' he said.

'I'm a mariner, not a tailor,' said Trask, 'but we have no choice.'

He brought the tiller back. The sail bellied as the wind filled it and they began moving more quickly toward the gut. Feet spread wide, Trask steered the ship to the centre of the channel. Then they were in it, the rock walls so close on either side that Brian felt he could reach out and touch them. Giles had gone forward too, carrying a spare yard that had been lying in the hold. They were almost through and could see the open water beyond the rocks when a wave picked them up and swung them toward the rock to starboard. Trask tried to bring the cog back but could not. As Brian moved toward Lianor, hoping to shield her when they crashed, Giles lifted the yard, put one end of it against the rock face and pushed. They could see the muscles bunch on his back and shoulders as, legs braced, he exerted all his enormous strength to fend them off. The yard snapped. He had not moved the ship more than a foot to port, but it was enough. They cleared the rock and then they were through the passage and out in the open waters beyond.

Lianor sighed and Brian realized that he had been holding his breath too.

'Well done,' he said to Trask.

'Well or ill, we've still our friends to reckon with,' said Trask.

Engrossed in the running of the narrow strait, they had forgotten the Moors, but now they all turned and looked astern. The freshening wind had cleared away most of the fog and now they could see the two huge rocks with the cleft between them very clearly. And on the far side, driving straight for the opening with drum beating and oars flashing, was the galley.

'But they can't get through that,' said Brian. For though the galley itself was much narrower than the *Swallow*, the oars extended out farther on either side than the width of the passage.

'If they're the seamen I think they are, they can,' said Trask. 'Watch.'

The galley was almost at the opening now, lifting to the drive of her oars at each stroke so that the metal ram at her bow showed above water. The captain, a swarthy man in a turban who stood at the tiller, shouted an order. The drum beat even more quickly then stopped abruptly and the slaves at the oars raised them and brought them into the ship's sides. Scarcely slackening its speed, the galley glided into the cleft between the rocks.

'Tertius. . .' said Lianor again.

'I don't know what I can do now,' he said, 'except . . . I may be able to keep them from boarding us.'

'How?'

Raising both his hands, he brought them around in a sweeping gesture and flames began to burn on the surface of the sea, surrounding them. Then, as suddenly as they had appeared, they went out.

'Keep trying,' said Lianor.

Again Tertius made the pass and again the flames flickered for a moment. Then, as before they went out.

'Ah, well,' said Hugh. 'It can't be easy to light a fire on the sea. But perhaps I can do something.'

The galley was more than halfway through the passage now, still moving quickly, and the Moors who lined its rails, ready to board them, began waving their curved swords and shouting. Hugh drew, held for a moment

50

and loosed smoothly. The arrow flew straight and true. The captain jerked upright, his hands going to the shaft in his chest, then fell sideways across the tiller, pushing it to port. The galley swerved. There was a rending crash as it ran into the rock on the starboard side, tipped and began to fill.

A cheer went up from the *Swallow's* crew.

'Well' said Trask, looking first at Hugh, then at Giles and Tertius, 'I wished for a company of archers, but we did none so ill with what we have on board.'

'I did nothing,' said Tertius.

'You freshened the wind and cleared away the fog,' said Lianor.

'In two tries. Besides I'm not sure I did it. It could well have happened anyway.'

'In any case we are, for the moment, safe,' said Trask. 'And if the wind and our luck hold I shall be able to put you ashore in the morning.'

Their luck did hold for they saw no other ships, friendly or otherwise. And the wind not only held but blew harder than ever, driving the *Swallow* on almost due east along the coast.

It was a wild and desolate coast with high cliffs rising from the sea and many rocks at their base and just off-shore. Brian wondered how they could land there, but when they woke the following morning they were sailing up a wide estuary with flat, marshy ground on either side of it.

'Right or left bank?' asked Trask.

'The right,' said Tertius. 'We will be going further down the coast.'

Trask nodded and, when they reached a place where the bank was high and firm, he put the *Swallow* alongside it and anchored. The gangplank was run out and the horses saddled and led ashore. They had all taken turns sitting with Merlin during the voyage, hoping—though they knew it was unlikely—that there might be some change. But when he was put on his litter and carried to the bank he was as still and rigid as ever.

"So this is France,' said Wat who had become himself when they reached the calm waters of the estuary. 'It looks no different from the Downs.'

'I think you will find it somewhat different,' said Trask. He had been uneasy since they anchored and was clearly anxious to get away. 'If you need nothing more we will go while the tide is still with us.' And when they had thanked him, 'There is no need for that. If you succeed in your mission I think we shall hear of it. And if you fail I'm sure we will.'

He went back on board. The gangplank was drawn in, the anchor raised and the sail unfurled and the *Swallow* glided away from the bank on the outgoing tide.

They watched her go until she was hidden by a curve in the estuary. And when she disappeared they felt, not only alone, but as if everything that was known and familiar had gone too.

6

'Which way?' asked Brian.

Tertius unrolled the map he had brought with him and studied it for a moment, then pointed south and east.

'That way,' he said.

'If we're looking for the tower we saw in the mirror, it was on the coast,' said Lianor.

'I know,' said Tertius. 'We'll reach the coast again further on.'

'Very well,' said Brian. He mounted Gaillard and the great white charger, happy to be on land again, reared playfully, tugging at the bit. Gracielle was restless too, dancing sideways as Lianor held her in.

'They need exercise,' said Brian. 'We'll ride ahead and spy out the land.'

'Good,' said Tertius. 'But keep within sight if not within hail. We're none too strong a fighting force as it is.'

Brian released Gaillard and he went into a canter with Gracielle running easily beside him. The ground sloped up from the marshy banks of the estuary and the two horses raced side by side until they reached the top of the rise and Brian and Lianor could see what lay beyond it. The country ahead was barren, dotted with gorse and heather and an occasional clump of scrubby, windswept pine. As far as they could see there was no sign of human habitation. But since Brian was not sure that those who lived there would be friendly, he was more pleased than disturbed by this.

Checking their horses, he and Lianor looked back. Tertius was leading the others up the hill, suiting the pace of his palfrey to that of the two horses that carried Merlin's litter. Giles had made Merlin his special charge and, since he and Migbeg had become good friends, the two of them walked beside the litter. Hugh, Hob and Wat, always the hunters, had spread out on either side of the line of march, their bows braced and ready. And even as Brian and Lianor watched a rabbit broke from cover ahead of Hob, scuttling for its burrow. Scarcely pausing, Hob whipped an arrow from his belt, nocked and loosed and the rabbit went head over heels in a cartwheel and lay still.

'Well,' said Brian as Hob picked it up, 'at least we shall not go hungry here.'

They waited until the others had joined them and then rode on again more sedately. By noon, though the country was as barren and empty as ever, it had become more rolling. They paused near a small stream, watered the horses and ate some bread and cheese. As they were about to go on, Migbeg whistled softly under his breath and pointed to a raven which had settled on a large stone nearby and was looking at them with bright and knowing eyes.

'That is no ordinary raven,' said Hugh.

'Few ravens are ordinary,' said Tertius, 'as few owls are.'

'I don't like the way he's studying us,' said Wat, taking an arrow from his belt. 'If he has come as a spy . . .'

'If he has,' said Lianor, 'he was not sent by an enemy.'

54

'How do you know?'

'I know,' she said with such assurance that Wat put back his arrow. The raven cawed hoarsely as if in acknowledgement, flapped its wings and rose into the air. It circled above them, then flew off in the direction they were going.

At dusk they made camp near a spring in a valley between two small hills. By this time Hugh and his men had collected a mixed bag of game including some heathcock and partridges as well as rabbits and Hob, who had been the outlaws' cook in the greenwood, made a savory stew out of these and some herbs he had picked during the day's march. It was dark when they had finished eating, and they were sitting around the fire debating whether they should take turns keeping watch during the night when Gaillard, grazing near the spring, raised his head and neighed.

They all leaped to their feet, reaching for their weapons, then paused as a strange and imposing figure came into the circle of firelight; a tall man wearing a long white robe. Though he was old—his hair and beard were as white as his robe—his back was straight and he walked with a firm and vigorous stride.

'Fear not,' he said. 'I come in peace.'

'Then you are welcome,' said Brian. 'May we ask who you are?'

'Venantius, Arch-Druid of Armorica. And you?'

Brian gave his name and those of all the others. And though Venantius nodded courteously to each of them, when Brian had finished he looked somewhat disappointed.

'And this is your whole company?'

'Why do you ask?'

'Because, while I would not misprize any here, word

came to me that one of the great ones of Britain was with you.'

'There is one more of us, Father,' said Tertius.

Taking a brand from the fire, he led the way to the litter which they had placed on the turf side on the far of their circle. The Druid looked down at the still figure and his face became bleak.

'Merlin himself,' he said. 'Who laid the spell on him? Was it Urlik?'

'Yes,' said Tertius.

'Then our plight is even worse than I feared. For if Merlin could not stand against him, who can?' Then, 'How did it happen?'

Tertius told him, telling him also why they had come to those parts and Venantius nodded.

'You should warn your king. He passed through here many weeks ago on his way to the south. If you go that way you should be able to find him.'

'We will find him,' said Brian. 'But what about Urlik? Can you tell us anything about him?'

'I can tell you a little,' said Venantius. 'What would you know?'

'Anything that might be useful to us,' said Tertius. 'For instance, is he here in Armorica?'

'Yes,' said Venantius. 'His stronghold is about two days march from here, further along the coast. Though I am not certain he is there now. At last report he was in the field with his general. For some of our people are still fighting him.'

'Is there any chance that they can defeat him?' asked Brian.

'None,' said the Druid flatly. 'They may hold out for a few more days—a week or so at most—but that is all.'

'And then what?'

'He will sail against Britain.'

'Is that certain?' asked Lianor.

'Yes, princess,' said Venantius as flatly as before. 'As soon as his horsemen arrived here, he began gathering together ships. He already has several hundred waiting in various places along the coast. Why else would he need them?'

'But if he has already conquered everything east of here why must he have Britain too?'

'Because if he does not take Britain he is not secure anywhere.'

'You are speaking militarily?'

'No. Though of course he cannot ignore a country which would serve as a haven and a base for any who oppose him. But it is not only plunder and territory that he wants. What he wants even more is to rule the hearts and minds of all men everywhere. And to do this he must take Britain.'

'I'm still not sure I understand why,' said Brian.

'Because of who and what he is,' said Tertius.

'Exactly,' said Venantius. 'He is the instrument, the agent of the Dark Powers. And from earliest times Britain has always been the sacred isle; the home, the font and source of white magic. Your groves and standing stones are the most hallowed of any, and it is there that we Druids have always gone to learn what we must to serve mankind and the One who is the Light as opposed to Urlik's darkness.'

'Then this is an even greater struggle than we thought,' said Brian.

'It is *the* struggle. It is one that has taken place before and will again whenever one age is ending and another is about to begin; the conflict that determines what the new age shall be. Your country is only part of the prize, but without it Urlik's crown will not rest easily on his brow and it will be missing its brightest jewel.'

'Is there anything you can do to help us?' asked Tertius.

'If Merlin and Blaise, who were both wiser and more powerful than I, could do nothing, what can I do?' said Venantius. 'I can only tell you that I think you are right in believing that our only hope lies in breaking the spell that was put on Merlin.'

'And do you know how that can be done?'

'No. I know something about Urlik's magic, as I think you do. He is a shaman, a traveller in the world of darkness, and as much at home there as he is here. I think he has taken Merlin to the place we Druids call Annwn. But I do not know how you can bring him back.'

'Is there no one who knows and could tell us?' asked Lianor.

'There might be one if she is permitted to.'

'She?'

'You know her?' said the Druid looking at her closely.

'Yes. I was not sure she was here too.'

'She is everywhere. And since tomorrow is the night of the full moon . . .'

Lianor nodded. 'Where can we find her?'

'A day's march from here that way.' He pointed south and east. 'If you know her you will know the place when you see it.'

'Yes,' said Lianor. 'Thank you.'

'It is I who thank you,' said Venantius, rising. 'For you have made me feel that all is not yet lost. There is one more thing that I can do. I can give you a word and a sign. I do not know how and when you will use them, but it comes to me that you should know them. To whom shall I give them?' He looked at Brian. 'You are a warrior. They are not for you.' He looked at Tertius. 'You have much knowledge, far more than I have, but it is a different kind of knowledge. And besides, you are not sure you believe in mine.' Finally he looked at Lianor. 'You know the White Lady. I think it should be you.'

'Very well, Father,' said Lianor.

'Here is the sign,' said Venantius. And taking a stone knife from his girdle he drew three lines on the hard packed earth; two straight and parallel and one at an angle to them. 'But do not inscribe it with metal. It is far older than metal. As for the word . . .' He leaned close to her and whispered in her ear. 'Will you remember it?'

'Yes, Father,' said Lianor.

'Good. May the Light shine on you and may you be as steadfast as oaks in the hour of trial.' He lifted his hand in blessing and then strode off into the darkness.

'So,' said Hugh. 'We know we have some friends here.'

'Some friends and many enemies,' said Tertius. 'But I do not think we need set a watch tonight.'

And so they set no watch but all slept—and soundly for they were tired after their long march that day.

The next day they were up with the sun and, after eating, continued on across the barren wasteland. Again that day they met no one but, as the sun began to sink, they saw a dolmen in the distance; two standing stones with a third stone lying across their tops.

'Let us camp here.' said Lianor.

They found a spring nearby, made a fire and ate and then stretched out on their cloaks to wait. The moon came up, bright and full, and when it was just above the capstone of the dolmen, Lianor rose and said, 'We can go now.'

Brian, Tertius and Migbeg got up also, but Hugh said, 'You may know this White Lady, princess, but I do not nor do I wish to. I will stay here.'

'And I,' said Hob.

'I too,' said Wat.

'If you think I should come with you, I will,' said Giles. 'If not, I will stay here with Merlin.'

'There is no need for you to come,' said Lianor. And so just the four of them went, with Lianor leading the way.

She led them towards the dolmen and then around it so that they approached it from the east. When they were some fifteen or twenty feet from it, Lianor checked them and bowed her head. Looking through the arch of the dolmen Brian could see the light of their campfire in the distance. An owl called softly from somewhere off to their right. Another answered it, nearer at hand and Brian suddenly realized it was Lianor who had responded. When he looked at the dolmen again their fire seemed to be dimming, becoming pale and steady instead of ruddy and flickering. Then all at once the Lady they had seen more than a year before out on the heath was standing between the upright stones.

As she had then, she seemed taller than a man and more beautiful than a mortal woman, though there was something cold about her beauty, like moonlight on freshly fallen snow. She wore the same long, shimmering robe that she had worn then and, as before, gems gleamed in her unbound hair like stars on a clear night.

'Greetings,' she said as they did her a deep reverence. 'So we meet again.'

'Yes, my lady,' said Lianor.

'You are all somewhat changed. You, my dear, have

become younger. You,' to Brian, 'older. And you,' to Tertius, 'have become wiser.'

'Very little wiser,' he said.

'It speaks well for you that you know that. But who is this other that you have brought with you?'

Migbeg murmured something in his own tongue and she said, 'Oh. Yes, of course.' Then, 'What can I do for you?'

'I think you know, my lady,' said Lianor.

'Yes. At least I know why you have come here. But this time I am not sure I can help you.'

'Then Venantius was right,' said Lianor. 'It is not permitted?'

'It was never permitted—not if it would change what is to be. And of course I know little more about that than you. Like the chronicler in his cell, I can but take note of what occurs, sometimes happily, but more often sadly.'

'And in this case?' asked Tertius.

'Need you ask that? You must know that I like Urlik no more than you. But if you learned anything from Merlin you must also know that night is as necessary as day. That if there were no Urliks there would be no need for Merlins or Arthurs.' She studied them a moment. 'Poor children, that does not content you, does it?'

'I am content, my lady,' said Brian. 'I am more than content merely to see you again.'

'That was gallantly said. It pleases me to hear it for I am not sure how much longer any will say it, here or elsewhere.'

'Oh, no!' said Lianor. 'That's impossible!'

'Not at all impossible, my dear. I have had a long day, longer than most, but it is almost over. Oh, I will not be forgotten completely. There will always be those who remember me. And while endings cannot be known, I think perhaps my day will come again. Meanwhile, because what you came here for was not for yourselves, let me see if there is anything at all I can do for you.'

She raised her hand and three small birds—chaffinches from their size—flew in out of the darkness and settled on her shoulder. Each in turn moved in close to her ear and seemed to whisper to her and she nodded.

'It seems that, as before, I can answer three questions for you. You do have questions?'

'Many questions,' said Tertius.

'Well, here are the answers: No. But nothing on earth or of the earth can kill him. Yes. When the stones march behind the banner of the king and past and future become one. And finally, by making a journey to the place to which none go willingly and from which few return unchanged.'

'But what are the questions?' asked Brian.

'No one could know them as well as you,' said the White Lady. 'And now I must go. I do not know if we shall meet again. But if we do not, I hope you will be among those who do remember me.' She looked at them a moment longer, then raised her hand again and a dark cloud moved in from the east, hiding the moon. When it had gone, she was gone too.

'It was good to see her again,' said Brian. 'But I must confess I hoped she could do more for us.'

'What more could she do?' asked Lianor. 'After all, she answered our questions for us.'

'But what were they?'

'As she said, if anyone should know, we should. What was yours?' she asked Tertius.

'It was about Urlik. I wondered if he were truly deathless.'

'That must have been the first question she answered. "No, but nothing on earth or of the earth can kill him." What was yours?' she asked Brian.

'I was thinking of what Venantius said about Urlik's armies and wondering if they could be defeated.'

'That was the second question she answered. "Yes. When the stones march behind the banner of the king and past and future become one." '

'What was your question?' Tertius asked her.

'The one I thought you would ask,' she said. 'How the spell on Merlin could be broken.'

' "By making the journey to the place to which none go willingly and from which few return unchanged!" '

'Yes,' said Brian. 'At least that's what she said. But do you know what any of it means?'

'No,' said Tertius. 'But I think that in time we may find out.'

7

Though Hob, Wat and Giles were asleep when they returned to camp, Long Hugh was not. He looked at the four curiously but did not ask any questions. This, Brian thought, was just as well since he was not sure he would have known how to answer even such a simple one as whether things had gone well or ill.

The next morning they went on again over the barren land, still meeting no one and seeing nothing except small game. Late in the afternoon they spied gulls wheeling and circling high in the air and knew they were drawing near the sea again. Then as the sun began to sink they saw some standing stones in the distance and made their way towards them. As they drew closer they saw that it was not just an isolated group of stones such as they had come across before, but that there were more of them— many more—than a man could count: an avenue of menhirs, eleven rows wide, running from west to east and extending as far as the eye could see.

They paused at the head of the avenue, looking down the lines of grey, lichen-covered stones that seemed to march in ranks towards the horizon and Long Hugh said, 'What is this place?'

'It is called Kerrec,' said Tertius.

'But who put up the stones and why?'

'I don't know,' said Tertius. 'I'm not sure anyone knows.'

'Well, I don't like it,' said Hugh. 'Are we going to camp here?'

'It's almost dusk,' said Giles. 'There's a spring over there and the horses are tired. I think perhaps we should.'

'Very well then,' said Hugh. 'But I still don't like it.'

Though the moor was bare and desolate they found enough brush to build a fire and cook their supper. After they had eaten, Giles and the outlaws huddled close to the blaze, but Brian, Lianor, Tertius and Migbeg walked back to the avenue of standing stones and a short way into it. The moon was still almost full and by its light they could see the rough texture of the stones, each standing taller than a man, and the small blue gentians that grew around and between them.

'A strange place,' said Brian. 'There's something here, some kind of power.'

Lianor and Tertius both nodded.

'Good or evil?' asked Brian.

'Not evil,' said Lianor.

'No,' said Tertius. 'I don't think so either. There are places where the oldest of magics, the earth magic that goes back beyond all memory, is still strong. This is one of them.'

They stood there a while longer and the longer they remained there the more conscious Brian became of the power that seemed, not only to surround them, but to press on them like a gentle but steady wind; a force that seemed to move along the lines of stones towards the east.

When they turned to go, Migbeg bent down, picked a handful of the blue gentians and placed them at the base of one of the largest stones. Somehow it seemed an appropriate gesture.

The next morning they found that they were, as they had thought, on the coast again. When they went on, they kept some distance inland on the high ground that ran parallel to the shore, for the coast was much indented and there were many bays that they would have had to go around. Several times they saw groups of ships anchored in the bays or drawn up close to shore in the coves and here they moved carefully, making sure they did not show themselves against the sky. For these, they were sure, must be the ships that Urlik had been gathering for his attack on Britain and it was likely that he had men guarding them.

Late in the afternoon they came to a pine wood and made their way through it. As they came to the far side of it Brian, who was leading them, paused and gestured to the others to be silent. When they moved up beside him they saw why. There, some three hundred yards away was the tower they had seen in the magic mirror; a tower that was the keep of a castle near the edge of a cliff.

'Is this the place we were looking for?' asked Hugh.

'Yes,' said Tertius. 'Urlik's stronghold.'

'A stronghold indeed,' said Hugh.

Studying it, Brian had to agree. It was not only formidable in itself, but its location made it almost impregnable. For it was set on a huge rock that was surrounded by the sea. The rock was some twenty or thirty feet from the edge of the cliff and since its sides were smooth and sheer, the castle could only be reached by its drawbridge which was now up.

'It seems undermanned,' said Lianor.

'It does,' said Brian, for only three or four men-at-arms stood on the parapet, keeping an indifferent watch. 'Most of the garrison must be away.'

Tertius had taken out the spyglass that he had had the goldsmith in Meliot make for him a year or more before and was examining the keep. Then he turned the glass towards the parapet and stiffened. A tall, slim woman in black had come out of the upper part of the gatehouse and was walking the ramparts. Even without Tertius' glass, both Brian and Lianor knew who she was.

'Nimue!' said Lianor.

'The enchantress who kept Merlin under a spell for so many years?' asked Giles.

'Who thought she had him under a spell,' said Tertius. 'We should have guessed that she would ally herself with Urlik. For she too wanted power and hated Merlin.'

'Now what?' asked Brian.

'You know why we came,' said Tertius.

'To get hold of that book of Urlik's and find out how he put the spell on Merlin.'

'Yes. But now that we're here I don't see how it can be done.'

'If you mean you want to get in there, it's impossible,' said Lianor.

'I'm not so sure,' said Brian, still studying the castle. 'If the rest of the garrison doesn't return before we're ready, I think it might be done.'

'How?' asked Lianor.

'It's a good bowshot,' said Brian to Hugh. 'Could you carry it from here?'

'Not with a fore-hand shaft, but I could carry it. And so could Hob and Wat.'

'And hit aught?'

'We could not promise to nail each finger of a glove in turn, but we could hit any reasonable mark.'

'By moonlight?'

'If there is light enough to see, why not?'

'Then this is how it could be done,' said Brian and he told them.

'You're mad!' said Lianor, going pale.

'It might work,' said Hugh. 'We could do our part.'

'I'd be willing to try it,' said Tertius.

'No!' said Lianor. 'It would mean certain capture or death. You can't do it!'

'As Tertius said, it's why we came here,' said Brian. 'We must try it.'

'No!' said Lianor again.

'Yes,' said Brian firmly. 'I didn't want you to come with us. If you hadn't come there would have been no argument about it. Let's have none now.'

'But there must be some other way. Think of what we'd be risking—not just you, but Tertius too. Without the two of you, what could we accomplish?'

'I don't know, but it's a chance we must take.'

Lianor still hesitated. Then, with an effort, 'Very well,' she said.

They moved back to a small clearing deeper in the wood where they unfastened Merlin's litter, laid it on the mossy ground and set the horses to grazing. Then they returned to the edge of the wood and ate a cold supper while watching the castle.

By dusk, though the guard on the battlements had changed, no one had entered the castle. It had been a heavy day and the dark clouds massing in the distance out to sea promised a storm. Brian thought it would hold off until after they had made their attempt, but Giles insisted that they cut pine boughs and make a shelter to protect Merlin in case he should be wrong.

They waited till the sun had set. Then, as it became dark, Brian rose.

'You'll be careful?' said Lianor drawing close to him.

'Of course,' he said. She held out her hand and he raised it to his lips.

Hugh, Hob and Wat moved off to the left to take their position and Brian led Tertius, Giles and Migbeg to the right. He paused when they came to a ridge that ran from the wood to the edge of the cliff where the draw-bridge came down. The moon had not yet come up and it took him a moment to get his bearings in the dark. Then he went on again, crouching low, keeping to the far side of the ridge and moving as quietly as possible with the others following him. Though Giles stumbled once the sound of the waves breaking far below them covered the noise and they reached the edge of the cliff safely. They took shelter behind a large rock and waited again, this time for the moon to rise.

The castle wall loomed over them on the far side of the chasm that separated it from the cliff. And though a few lights showed in the windows of the keep, the battlements were so dark that they could not tell if any kept watch there. Then the moon came up, shining brightly for, in spite of the clouds to the west, the sky overhead was still clear. When it was high enough so that they could make out the shape of the stones in the bailey wall, Brian whis-tled softly and rapidly like a curlew. He was immedi-ately answered by an owl's hoot from the edge of the wood.

A man-at-arms stepped out of the upper part of the gatehouse and began walking the battlements towards the far corner. As he paused, looking casually towards the wood, there was a faint flicker in the moonlight and he cried out and fell back out of sight with an arrow through his shoulder.

There were shouts and the sound of running feet as other guards came hurrying to the aid of the wounded man and a hail of arrows whistled from the wood, coming so fast that it was as if at least a dozen archers were hidden there.

There was silence for a moment, then Nimue herself appeared on the ramparts near the keep. She too looked towards the wood, then turned and called an order to someone below in the inner bailey.

'I think she's going to do it,' whispered Tertius.

Brian nodded. There was a clanking from inside the gatehouse as the portcullis was raised, then a rumble and a jarring thud as the drawbridge came down. Migbeg stirred and Brian put a restraining hand on his arm. Then the gates opened and a party of mounted men-at-arms came out for a sortie. There were perhaps two dozen of them, stout varlets in leather jacks and steel caps. Their captain, a heavy set man on a shaggy pony, had long, dark mustachios, yellowish skin and strangely slanted eyes. He led them across the drawbridge and up towards the wood at a gallop.

'Now!' said Brian and he rose from behind the rock and ran across the drawbridge with the others behind him. When the sallying party had left the castle, the portcullis had been dropped again, but Brian had expected this. He ran to the right, around the projecting tower of the gatehouse to where it joined the outer wall. Picking up Migbeg as if he were a child, Giles held him high against the wall. Migbeg felt for a foothold, found it, then was up the wall like a cat. Reaching the rampart on top, he uncoiled the rope he had wrapped around his waist and lowered it. Now Giles picked up Brian and set him on his shoulders. With the help of the rope he too climbed the wall and he and Migbeg together pulled Tertius up after them.

Leaning over the parapet, Brian waved to Giles and the giant nodded and ran back across the drawbridge, disappearing behind the rock.

Now, for the first time, Brian looked around. Nimue was at the far corner of the ramparts with four men-at-arms, looking up towards the wood. Brian looked that way too. The mounted party, met by a storm of arrows, had paused half way to the wood and was now riding parallel to it, trying to keep a safe distance from it. Even as Brian watched one of the men-at-arms threw up his arms and fell from his horse with an arrow through his chest.

Brian turned back to Tertius and Migbeg.

'Now what?' he asked.

'The keep,' said Tertius.

Migbeg had tied the rope around one of the merlons and was dropping it down the outside of the wall. Brian drew Starflame, the sword he had found in the howe when they had first met Migbeg, and the three of them ran crouching along the ramparts to the tower. They went in and paused on the spiral stairs. A torch burned on the wall and opposite them was a heavy oaken door. Tertius tried it, but it was locked.

'Up or down?' asked Brian.

'Down first,' said Tertius and he led the way down the stairs.

When they reached the bottom they found themselves in the great hall. It was large, almost as large as the great hall in the palace at Meliot. At the far end of it was a dais with three thrones on it and a tall lancet window behind them. Two of the thrones were wooden and plain but the one in the centre was iron and curiously wrought for its arms were two dragons with open mouths and

71

staring eyes; the dragons' wings made its back and its legs were the legs of the dragons.

The room was dim, lit only by the moonlight that came in through the tall, narrow window and in that light the iron dragons seemed almost to be alive, watching them balefully.

Tertius looked at the iron throne and around the hall, then went back up the stairs again. The heavy oak door on the floor above was still closed and Tertius went past it and on up. On the floor above was another door. Tertius tried this, it opened and they went in. This room was small and bare, little larger than a monk's cell A tall, black candle burned on a low chest. Next to it, in the corner, was a pallet with a figure lying on it. Migbeg hissed softly in warning, but Tertius walked over to the pallet and they followed him. The man lying there was the old, white haired man they had seen in the magic mirror.

'Blaise,' said Brian.

Tertius nodded. Like Merlin, Blaise lay still and stiff, looking up with open but unseeing eyes.

'Shall we take him with us?' asked Brian.

'No. It would do no good,' said Tertius.

He looked down sadly at the elderly magician who had been Merlin's teacher, then turned and left the room. Again he led them up the stairs, trying each door as they came to it and glancing within.

'If you're looking for the room we saw in the mirror,' said Brian, 'it's probably the one below, the one that was locked.'

'Probably,' said Tertius.

But he still went up. They opened a last door and came out on top of the tower. Brian went to the parapet and looked down. Nimue had disappeared, but the four men-at-arms were still crouched in the far corner of the ramparts, looking towards the wood. Three more of the mounted men lay on the moonlit open ground with arrows in them. The others were sitting their horses about a quarter of a mile from the castle and well away from the wood while their captain harangued them. He was apparently trying to rally them for one more attempt to rout out the hidden bowmen, but having little success. From this height Brian could see behind the rock where they had hidden and saw that Giles was gone. He had, Brian hoped, been able to make this way back to the woods and rejoin the others.

He turned back to Tertius who was looking, not down but out to sea where the heavy storm clouds were moving closer. There was a distant rumble of thunder and Tertius started.

Brian went towards him, stumbling over a rusty chain that had probably been used to haul up the stones that lay there in piles ready to be dropped on any besiegers. Tertius looked at the chain and then at Migbeg.

'Migbeg,' he said, 'I need a sword. Will you give me yours?'

Migbeg hesitated. His sword was the one Brian had given him after Brian had found Starflame in the burial mound and it was precious to him. But he knew that Tertius was aware of that and would not ask him for it unless he had a compelling reason. So nodding, he drew the sword from his belt and gave it to him.

'Thank you,' said Tertius. He went to the inner wall of the parapet and glanced down. Then drawing his dagger he dug the mortar from between two stones, took Migbeg's sword and jammed the pommel into the crack with the blade pointing up.

'What are you doing?' asked Brian.

'I don't know if it will work,' said Tertius, 'so I'd rather not say.'

Picking up the rusty chain, he forced the end link over the sword blade and dropped the rest of the chain over the parapet so that it hung down the outside of the tower.

'Is it some kind of magic?' asked Brian.

'You could call it that,' said Tertius. 'And now we'd better go.'

They went down the stairs again, going quietly but more quickly this time and not pausing until they reached the door of the room over the great hall. The torch still burned in the bracket on the wall, but now the door was not closed but partly open.

Motioning them to be quiet, Tertius tiptoed over to it and looked in. And standing behind him, Brian and Migbeg looked in also. The room was the one they had been looking for—the one they had seen in the mirror. There were the shelves of books and the large one with the locks and clasps on the stand. In the far corner of the room was an oval mirror, the twin of the one that Merlin and Tertius had used. And standing in front of the mirror with her back to them was Nimue.

In the mirror they could see a vast encampment; hundreds of curious greyish tents with fires burning in front of them, and standing or sitting about the fires many hundreds of heavy-set, yellow skinned men like the captain of the sallying party. Nimue adjusted the mirror and Urlik himself appeared in it. He was inside one of the tents talking to another of the dark-haired, yellow-skinned men, one of his generals from his bearing and rich dress.

'Urlik . . . Master . . .' said Nimue.

Urlik lifted his head as if he were listening. He took a

small mirror from inside his robe and held it up. He apparently could hear her now as well as see her for Nimue began speaking to him quickly and urgently. Brian could not hear what she was saying, but Urlik frowned. Then he looked past her, stiffened and said something to her, pointing.

Nimue turned and saw them standing there just outside the partly open door. As she did, Tertius pushed the door open wider, stepped into the room and made a quick pass with each hand at the mirror. Urlik was trying to say something more, but the mirror became dim and cloudy and his face disappeared.

'So,' said Nimue. 'The young wizard and his friend.'

'Yes, Nimue,' said Tertius.

'I wondered who was besotted enough to attack the castle and why. Now I know.'

'Do you?'

'Perhaps not everything. But it does not matter. Because now that you are here, you shall stay here. And you will tell me.'

She started to raise her hand but Tertius made a rapid gesture, saying something under his breath, and she froze, looking startled.

'Well,' she said. 'You have grown in power since I last saw you.'

'Why should you be surprised when for almost a year I have had for my master the man who taught you all you know?'

'Merlin?' She laughed. 'How long did he stand against my new master? And where is he now? Lying senseless in his tower like that other dotard upstairs.'

'Are you sure, Nimue?'

'You mean he is not?' She was still struggling to raise her hand. 'Then why are you here?' She glanced at the book on the stand near the table. 'Ah, of course. Urlik's Grimoire. You do not know how to lift the spell. And you never will know.'

'Again, do not be too sure, Nimue.' Her hand was almost up but Tertius made another pass, checking it. 'We will go now. But I think we will meet again.'

He stepped backward out of the room and closed the door. The key was in the lock and he turned it, locking the door from the outside.

'You did well,' said Brian.

'No,' said Tertius. 'I never did get to see the book. Now we'd best go quickly. It won't take her long to break that binding spell and give the alarm.'

They hurried back out on to the ramparts. As they ran toward the gatehouse they heard horses' hoofs on the drawbridge and, glancing over the battlements, Brian saw that the sallying party had returned. There were only about a dozen of them left. The rest of them, including the captain, lay on the open ground between the castle and the wood with arrows in them. Then the portcullis came crashing down and with a rattling, creaking noise the drawbridge started to go up.

'We're too late,' said Tertius with some dismay. 'Now what?'

'Down the rope,' said Brian. 'I'll join you in a little while.'

'But if the drawbridge is up . . .'

'Go ahead!' said Brian.

Obediently Tertius climbed over the parapet and slid down the rope. It was much darker now as the storm clouds moved in overhead. Continuing on, Brian pushed open the door of the gatehouse and went in. The four men-at-arms who had been on the ramparts were there working the winch that raised the drawbridge. They looked up startled and reached for their swords, but Brian struck the nearest one on the side of the head with the flat of his blade and he fell down senseless. The others looked past Brian and fled out the other door. Glancing back, Brian saw that Migbeg had followed him. Though he no longer had a sword, his stone axe was in his hand.

'I meant you to go down the rope too,' said Brian. Then, as Migbeg shook his head and held up his axe, 'Well, as always, you were a help.'

He pushed forward the lever that engaged the drum of the winch, and the drawbridge went rattling and rumbling down. Then he and Migbeg went running back to the rope and slid down it to the ground.

The storm was on them now and the rain began coming down as they raced across the drawbridge and toward the shelter of the wood. An arrow whistled by Brian's head, so close he could feel the wind of it, then another. Then, as a flight of arrows came from the wood, forcing the archers on the castle wall to take cover, there was a drumming of horses' hoofs and out of the darkness came Lianor on Gracielle, leading Gaillard.

She checked the horses and Brian saw that she had already picked up Tertius and that he sat behind her. Mounting Gaillard, Brian pulled Migbeg up and then they were away, galloping toward the wood.

'I told you to stay with Hugh and the others,' said Brian. 'Why did you do this?'

Leaning well forward on Gracielle, who was running neck and neck with Gaillard, she looked sideways at him but did not even bother answering.

8

Giles was waiting for them at the edge of the wood and they went with him to the clearing where they had left Merlin. When the others joined them under the shelter they had made earlier, Brian said, 'That was well done, Hugh.'

'Not too ill. Though I'll confess you set our hearts crossways when we saw the drawbridge going up and you not yet back on this side of it. But did you accomplish what you set out to do?'

'No,' said Tertius.

'Well, sometimes we need a trial arrow or two before we strike the mark. But what now?'

'You can't go in there again,' said Lianor.

'No,' agreed Brian. 'We had an encounter with Nimue. And while Tertius outfaced her, she knows that we are here and so does Urlik. We must leave before he comes back with the castle garrison or an even larger force.'

'And go where?' asked Lianor.

'I don't know,' said Tertius, 'since I don't know what our next move should be.'

'Perhaps we should sleep on it,' said Giles. 'As my sister says, "Only an owl sees more clearly at midnight than at dawn."'

Brian felt that they were safe at least until morning so

they made themselves as comfortable as they could under the roof of pine boughs. Wrapping themselves in their cloaks, Brian and Lianor sat with their backs against a tree somewhat apart from the others so that they could talk. And when Lianor fell asleep, it was with her head on his shoulder.

The rain stopped during the night and the morning was bright and clear. They did not take the time to build a fire but broke their fast on bread and cold meat and then left the wood, going inland, away from the castle and the coast.

They had not gone more than a half mile or so when Migbeg whistled softly, pointing south. Shading his eyes, Brian looked that way and saw the glint of steel.

'He's right,' he said. 'I see lances.'

'Many?' asked Tertius.

The ground was rolling and for a moment none of them could see more than the tips of the lances. Then horsemen began appearing on top of one of the low hills in the distance.

'Yes,' said Brian. 'At least five score.'

'Well,' said Hugh, bracing his bow, 'we had a busy night and now it seems we shall have a busy morning.'

'I don't think it's Urlik,' said Brian. 'He was north of us last night and this company comes from the south. Besides, I think these are knights.' For now he could see the gleam of their armour.

'Still it's just as well to be ready,' said Hob, nocking an arrow.

Tertius, meanwhile, had taken out his spyglass and levelled it.

'No,' he said, smiling oddly. 'It's not Urlik.'

'Then who is it?' asked Brian.

'See for yourself,' said Tertius, handing him the glass.

Brian raised it and looked at the standard that one of the knights in the vanguard had unfurled; a white banner with a red dragon rampant.

'The king's banner!' he said.

'Yes,' said Tertius. 'It's Arthur. But do you see who's with him?'

Two knights had left the company and were cantering over the heath towards them. Brian turned the glass on them. One of them was young, broad shouldered and had a pleasant open face. But the other . . .

'My father!'

Tossing the spyglass back to Tertius, he touched Gaillard with his heels and went galloping to meet them.

They met almost midway between the two groups.

'Greetings, father,' said Brian, reining in.

'I thought I recognized Gaillard,' said Sir Owaine, smiling. Then more gravely, 'What do you here, Brian?'

'It is a long tale and a grim one. Is the king with you?'

'Yes.'

'Then since it concerns him and Britain perhaps we should wait until he joins us.'

'Perhaps,' said Sir Owaine. Then looking past Brian, 'But who do you have with you? Is that Tertius?'

'Yes. Tertius, Lianor and some friends.'

'Lianor?' Sir Owaine looked startled. 'Well, I suppose that is part of your tale. But I forget my manners.' He turned to the young knight who was with him. 'Sir Constantine, this is my son, Brian.'

'So I gathered,' said Sir Constantine holding out his hand. 'Greetings, Sir Brian.'

'My greetings to you, Sir Constantine,' said Brian, looking at him with interest. For Sir Constantine was the son of Cador, Duke of Cornwall, who was Arthur's cousin.

By now the company of knights had reached them and leading them was Arthur. Brian had never seen him before but he would have known him even without the blazon on his shield or the banner that floated over his head. Though of no more than average height, his kingship, which he wore as casually as his old campaigning cloak, made him seem taller than any of the knights who rode with him. He was no longer young—there was grey in his short beard—but his eyes were bright and clear and he sat his black charger easily.

'Well, Sir Owaine,' he said, 'you seem to have met a friend.'

'More than a friend, Sire. This is my son, Brian.'

'Ah. It's truly a happy meeting then. Greetings, Sir Brian. I have heard much of you.'

'If it was from my father, Your Majesty, I am sure you made the proper allowances.'

'I have never known Sir Owaine to say aught that was not true in every particular,' said Arthur smiling. 'But who are these others who are with you?'

Brian turned. Lianor, Tertius and the others had now joined them also and were gathered behind him.

Brian made them known one by one and the king greeted each of them with the same great courtesy, showing no surprise at Lianor's attire or Giles' size.

'But that is still not all,' he said. 'Who is that on the litter?'

'One you know, Your Majesty,' said Tertius, 'and part of the reason we are here.'

Arthur glanced at him, edged his horse closer to the litter and, 'Merlin!' he said.

'Yes, Sire.'

'He is not dead?'

'No, Sire. Under a spell.'

Again the king looked at Tertius. Then, 'I see we must talk.' He dismounted and when Brian, Lianor and Tertius had done so also, 'Tell me,' he said.

And so they did, Brian and Lianor beginning the tale and Tertius finishing it.

Arthur was silent for a moment when they were done.

'Though it was not unexpected, this is a dark and woeful day,' he said.

'You knew about Urlik, Sire?' asked Tertius.

'Yes. Merlin told me years ago that one day he would be a great threat to us. He was not sure when, but he did not want me to come here to France. This must have been why. And this must also have been why he sent me a message to return home.'

'When was this, Sire?'

'Some four days ago.'

'But it is almost a fortnight since Urlik laid the spell on him,' said Brian.

'Then who sent the message?'

'Who brought it?' asked Tertius.

'Why, I don't know,' said Arthur. 'Do you know, Sir Owaine?'

'No Sire. You were alone in your tent. When you came out you said you had received an urgent message to return home and that we were leaving in the morning.'

'It was not in writing then?' asked Tertius.

'No,' said Arthur. 'At least . . . You think it was Urlik?'

'Yes,' said Tertius. 'He must have put in it your mind that you had received a message. We suspected from the beginning that the attack of the Moors was part of his plot, a way of drawing you from England. What you thought was a message was another part of that plot, designed to separate you from your army.'

82

'I did not like it,' said Sir Owaine. 'Even though I did not know of this Urlik, a hundred knights did not seem enough to protect Your Majesty.'

'If Urlik's forces are as large as our friends here tell us, then all the men we have would not be enough,' said Arthur.' He looked at the litter again. 'Poor Merlin. He knew much. He knew he would be ensorcelled by Nimue and return. And he knew of the danger from Urlik. But he did not know everything. He did not know how this would come out.'

'He was not alone in that, Sire,' said Lianor. 'But two nights ago someone even wiser than Merlin told us that endings cannot be known.'

'Perhaps it is just as well,' said Sir Owaine. 'No man should ever think that what he does will not matter. But what will you do now, Sire?'

'What I set out to do,' said Arthur. 'Go on.'

'But, Sire, if this is part of Urlik's plot . . .'

'He does not know if it will succeed any more than we do. And if Britain is threatened, that is where I belong.'

'But should we not at least wait for the rest of our forces? They are not more than a day's march behind us.'

'How will a few thousand men-at-arms help us if Urlik has many times that? Still they must be warned. You will ride back, Sir Owaine, and tell the Duke of Cornwall what has happened and have him come on with all possible speed.'

'Nay, Sire,' said Sir Owaine. 'My place is here with you. Cannot Sir Constantine go? The Duke is his father . . .'

'If aught should happen to me, Cador will be king and I would like him to have the benefit of your counsel as I have had it.'

'But, Sire,' began Sir Owaine. Arthur looked at him and he broke off. 'It shall be as you say, Your Majesty.' Then turning to Brian, 'No matter what befalls, guard the king as I would—with your life!'

'Need you put even more of a burden on him?' asked Arthur. 'Has he not done enough already?'

'I have done naught, Sire,' said Brian.

'You and your friends have done a great deal,' said Arthur. Then looking at Lianor, Tertius and the others, he smiled. 'It is in my mind that I cannot blame Urlik overmuch.'

'How so, Your Majesty?'

'Who are your friends who came here with you to try and help me? A princess dressed as a squire, an apprentice magician, a giant, a Pict and three bowmen. Or should I say three outlaws? Not that it matters,' he said as Long Hugh dropped his eyes. 'If we come through this you shall be outlaws no longer. Now where else but in Britain could one assemble such a company? And who would not be ruler of such a country?'

'It is because we would have none but you as our king that we came, Your Majesty,' said Hugh.

'That I know, Hugh. But I thank you for saying it. Now you had best be off, Sir Owaine.'

'Yes, Your Majesty,' said Sir Owaine. And mounting, he raised his lance in salute and went galloping off toward the south.

'Do we go north then, Sire?' asked Sir Constantine when the king had mounted also.

'I think we should start that way,' said Arthur. 'Though it may be that we shall have to change our course like a prudent mariner when we sees storm clouds gathering. Do you know where Urlik is now?' he asked Brian.

'I think north and east,' said Brian. 'At least that is where he was last night.'

'I do not like trying to avoid him, but I suppose we must.'

'I'm not sure you'll be able to, Your Majesty,' said Hugh. 'Look.'

They looked in the direction he was pointing and there, silhouetted against the sky on a distant ridge was one of Urlik's horsemen on a shaggy pony. Even as they watched, he turned and went galloping off, disappearing behind the ridge.

'Wait,' said Arthur as both Brian and Sir Constantine started to go after him. 'I have heard of these Mongol ponies. You could never catch him.'

'But if he is one of Urlik's scouts and tells him you are here, Sire . . .' said Sir Constantine.

'If Urlik is the wizard he is said to be, he must know it anyway. So now it is not a matter of which way we will go but where we will go. Is there any place in these parts where we can make a stand, Sir Brian?'

Brian and Tertius looked at one another.

'Kerrec,' said Tertius.

'Yes,' said Brian slowly. 'I think that is the best place.'

'Can we be there by nightfall?'

'Yes, Sire.'

'Then take up your friends who are not mounted and show us the way.'

Brian took up Migbeg behind him, Lianor took Hugh and Tertius and Sir Constantine took Hob and Wat. This left Giles.

'Fear not, Your Majesty,' he said as Arthur looked at him uncertainly. 'Unless you go at a full gallop all the way you shall not leave me far behind.'

They set out, going north up the coast. Though they

rode steadily, they never went faster than a trot because of the pack horses and the horses that carried Merlin's litter. And with his long legs Giles was able to keep up with them easily.

Several times during the day they saw Urlik's horsemen in the distance keeping watch on them. And though each time Brian, Sir Constantine and others of the knights wanted to pursue them, Arthur always restrained them.

Shortly before dusk they reached Kerrec. They approached it from the east and the standing stones were casting long shadows as they rode up the hill that led to it and drew rein at the end of the avenue.

'A strange place,' said Arthur looking at the menhirs that stood one behind the others like files of stone giants, stretching on across the high ground until they disappeared in the distance. 'It is not what I expected, but it is a good place for a stand. The stones will give us some protection and the ground is in our favour.'

'That is what I thought, Sire,' said Brian. 'If Urlik attacks us it will be uphill. And if we attack it will be downhill.'

'You have your father's eye. But,' turning to Tertius, 'it was you who suggested it first.'

'For other reasons, Sire. There is a prophesy about this place. At least it could be about it.'

'What prophesy is that?'

'A few nights past we met one not far from here who answered some questions for us.'

'Who was that? A Druid?'

'No. Though it was a Druid who sent us to her.'

'Her?'

'Yes. It was the White Lady.'

Frowning a little, Arthur nodded. 'I have heard of her. What were the questions she answered?'

86

'One was about Urlik and whether his armies could be defeated. And the answer was, "Yes. When the stones march behind the banner of the king and past and future become one".'

Arthur glanced up at the dragon standard that Sir Constantine carried and which now fluttered over his head.

'Well, the banner is here and there are the stones. But how can they march?'

'They might be made to, Sire?' said Tertius.

'By magic?'

'Yes, Sire.'

'That would be a sight worth seeing. You will attempt it?'

'If there is need for it, yes, Sire.'

'Then perhaps you should get ready, Tertius,' said Brian.

He had been looking the other way while they talked. Now the king and Tertius turned and saw what he had seen: Mongol horsemen coming around the shoulder of the plateau that lay a mile or so to the east, not by the dozens or the hundreds, but by the thousands.

The king looked at them, then at the setting sun and said, 'It will soon be dark. They will not attack now. They will camp and wait until morning.'

Even as he said this, a horn blew and the horsemen began dismounting, unsaddling their horses and setting up the strange grey tents that Brian and Tertius had seen in Nimue's mirror.

'They are made of felt and called yurts,' said Arthur.

'You know a good deal about them, Sire,' said Tertius.

'I had little schooling when I was young. But later I had the best of all teachers, your master, Merlin. Let us camp too.'

And he led the way in among the standing stones.

They built fires and cooked food, the knights sitting in small groups and talking quietly. Like a good commander, Arthur walked about, exchanging a few words with this group, drinking some wine with another. Finally he came over to where Brian, Lianor and Tertius were sitting near the litter and looked down at Merlin.

'He still sleeps soundly. Do you think he dreams?'

'If he does, they are not bad dreams,' said Tertius. For Merlin's face was, as it had been, calm and expressionless.

'I do not grudge him his rest. He has worried long about many things. And while he was not alone in that, it is only right that the matter of Britain should be in my hands now.'

As he turned away, Brian said, 'Sire, may we speak with you?'

'Of course. Here?'

'It might be best if it were private.'

Arthur glanced at him, at Lianor and Tertius and then nodded.

'I can see that it might. Come then.'

They went with him up the avenue of standing stones to its end where they could look down at the fires in the Mongol camp.

'Do you think Urlik is there, Brian?'

'Yes, Sire. If Nimue's mirror did not lie, he was with his army last night.'

'I think he is there too. At what do you put his strength?'

'Not less than five thousand men.'

'Certainly not less than that and perhaps more. And we are just over a hundred. The odds against us are long.'

'Yes, Sire.'

'Is that what you wished to speak to me about?'

'Yes, Sire.'

'I thought so. Say on.'

Brian glanced at Lianor and Tertius, but since he had begun, he continued.

'Sire, there is no need to speak of what it would mean to Britain if you were captured or killed.'

'It would be a blow. Perhaps even a great blow,' said Arthur.

'It would be more than that, Your Majesty,' said Tertius. 'It would be one she could not survive.'

'It is one she will have to survive one day. Well?'

'Sire, it is a dark night. The standing stones run westward for at least two miles and give some cover. It was our thought that you could ride to the far end of the avenue and then, with one of us to guide you, make your way in secret to the north and thence back to England.'

'Again that was what I thought was in your mind,' said the king, smiling. 'Which one of you would go with me?'

'I, Sire,' said Lianor.

'You would leave Sir Brian?'

'Not willingly, Sire. But we agreed that since I would be of little use in the battle tomorrow, it would be better if I went than any of the others.'

'I thank you for your offer, princess, for I know that it would not be easy for you to go.'

'Then you will do it, Sire?' asked Brian.

'First let me ask you a question. If you were Urlik and were so anxious to take a fox named Arthur that you worked out a great strategem involving magic, alliances and the movement of whole armies—and if you finally ran him to earth, would you leave his bolt holes unguarded?'

89

'You mean that he must have horsemen watching all about us? That is likely, Sire. But there is a chance that you could get by them.'

'When he is a wizard too? Do you not think he would know by his black arts if I tried to leave here?'

'Perhaps. But again there is a chance that you could get away.'

'I will grant that. I asked you what you would do if you were Urlik. Now let me ask you what you would do if you were Arthur. Would you leave here?'

Brian looked at him, then at Lianor and Tertius.

'Do not look at your friends, Brian,' said the king. 'Look at me and answer me truthfully.'

'No, Sire,' said Brian. 'I would not.'

'Why?'

'Because even though I knew it would be my duty to save my life and return to Britain if it were possible, I could not leave my comrades-at-arms.'

'You have more than your father's eye. You have his honesty too. But if you would not leave why should I do so?'

'Because you should, Sire. I answered as I did because I am not a king and cannot think like a king.'

'It is not easy to think like a king,' said Arthur. 'I cannot always do it myself.'

'You did not ask me what I would do, Sire,' said Tertius.

'No, Tertius, I did not. Your view, like Merlin's, would be a large one and I think you would go. And while I honour you for it and suspect that that is what I should do, I will not go.'

'But why, Sire?' asked Lianor.

'Because, in the end, it does not matter.'

'It does not matter if you are taken or killed?'

'No, Brian. I told you before that I had learned much from Merlin. One of the things I learned is that I am nothing.'

'Sire!'

'It's true. It was not an easy thing for me to learn and it took me many years to learn it, but in the end I did. And when I had, I found that there was a certain peace in it.'

'But how can that be true, Sire? You are Arthur, our king! We have never had a king like you . . .'

'No,' said the king. 'And it is likely that there will not be another such for many years. But if I am aught, it is not because I am Arthur, but because I am the king and living now. Do you understand what I am saying, Tertius?'

'I think so, Sire. I think that what you are saying is that it is not the man—or the king—who makes the times, but the times that make the man.'

'You have been well taught,' said Arthur. 'Exactly so. In times like these—times of conflict and change—there are always those who have important parts to play. Who they are does not matter. All that matters is whether they play those parts well or ill.'

'And would it be failing in that part if you were able to return to Britain and continue to lead your people in this fight?' asked Lianor.

'That is a searching question, princess, and the answer is no. Though as yet I do not know all that is required of me, I believe I could go and do well or stay and do badly. But since there is a choice, I choose to stay.'

'And that is your final word, Sire?' asked Brian.

'Yes, Brian. Besides,' and he smiled, 'do you think I would miss the sight that has been promised us—that of seeing these stones march?'

'I did not promise that, Sire,' said Tertius. 'I said I would try and make them do so.'

'It seems I have more faith in you and your master than you have in yourself.' Then, turning back to Brian, 'Will you forgive me, Brian?'

'For what, Sire?'

'For doing what I am doing. As Merlin said to me many times, Kings and bears often worry their keepers.'

'Who am I to forgive you, Your Majesty?'

'A true knight who shall ride knee to knee with me tomorrow. May you rest well until then, all three of you.' And he walked back through the standing stones towards the fire.

9

The next morning dawned bright and clear with a light breeze blowing from the northwest. Brian had slept badly, waking several times during the night. And each time that he woke he found that Tertius was awake also. The first time, though it was too dark to see his face, he sensed that Tertius' eyes were open and that he was staring into the darkness. The next time he was sitting up with his back against one of the stones and sitting thus, he looked very small and very lonely.

Unwrapping his cloak, Brian went over to him.

'Why aren't you asleep?' he asked.

'Probably for the same reason you aren't.'

'You're worried about tomorrow?'

'Yes. The king is counting on me, Brian.'

'Not counting on you. He hopes that you can help us, but that is all.'

'And if I can't?'

Brian shrugged.

'Don't do that. Tell me what will happen if I cannot do anything to help?'

'I am afraid that will be the end, Tertius.'

'Yes. And not just of Arthur but of many things. Do you wonder then that I cannot sleep?'

'No, Tertius. You said in the beginning that the

responsibility for what happened on this mission was mostly yours. But you also said that, since there was no one else, you would take it on.'

'I know.'

'And I know that this is a bad time for you. But I also know that you will do what you can tomorrow. And no one can do more than that.'

'I suppose not.'

'Then will you sleep now?'

'Will you?'

'I'm going to try.'

'All right. So will I. Goodnight, Brian.'

'Good night,' said Brian and he went back to where he had been lying and wrapped himself in his cloak again.

But he did not sleep, for the thought of the morrow weighed heavily on him. Was this to be the end—for Arthur, Britain and all of them? He could imagine death. It would be a kind of sleeping. But he could not imagine a world in which all he knew and loved no longer existed. Was that the way it was to be?

Lianor, lying next to him, stirred in her sleep.

'No,' she whispered. 'No.'

'Lianor,' he said softly.

'No,' she said again.

He looked at her. Her face had been frowning, troubled. But, as he watched, it became calm.

You're right, he thought. It cannot end that way. And he closed his eyes.

When he woke next the sun was beginning to edge the hills to the west with pale light. He sat up. Lianor and Tertius were still asleep and so were most of the knights, all of them stretched out among the stones close to the embers of the fires. But the king was not asleep. His cloak lay on the ground near Sir Constantine, but he was standing at the end of the avenue of menhirs, looking down the long hill toward the Mongol camp. Getting up quietly so as not to disturb the others, Brian joined him.

'Good morrow to you, Brian,' said Arthur turning and smiling at him. 'I trust you slept well.'

'I cannot say I did, Sire.'

'Oh? I always slept well when I was your age, even before a battle. Now I sleep little at any time. But though we are about early, so are our friends.'

Looking down at the enemy camp, Brian saw that the Mongols were astir also, a few of them building up the fires while the rest were tending and saddling their horses.

'Shall I rouse the others, Sire?'

'It might be best. But since they seem to be getting ready to break their fast, I think we shall have time to do so also.'

By the time Brian and the king had returned, the others were up and about also. They ate quickly and then the king sent Hob and Wat to watch the Mongols while the rest of them gathered about him, the knights standing around him in a circle some six or eight deep.

'Do you have a plan of battle, Sire?' asked Sir Constantine.

'Yes,' said Arthur. 'But it depends in part on our young wizard here.' And he turned to Tertius. 'What think you about the stones now, Tertius?'

'I have been thinking about them most of the night, Sire,' said Tertius somewhat wryly. 'And while I know what should be done, I am not sure I can do it.'

'Is there aught we can do to help you?'

'No, Sire. There is only one man who could help me. No, not help me but do it as easily as I could pick one of those gentians. But of course he cannot.'

'Merlin.'

'Yes.'

'Well, if we cannot help you we shall leave you to do what you can.' He turned back to Brian, Sir Constantine and his knights. 'Since our position is good, if our strength were anywhere near that of Urlik, I would wait for his attack. But since it is not, we shall not wait. When his forces have arrayed themselves, we shall attack.'

'That likes me well, Sire,' said Sir Constantine, and the knights murmured their assent. 'No matter what comes of it we shall give a good account of ourselves.'

'Of that I am sure. Brian, you will ride on my right and Sir Constantine on my left. We will lead the charge. The rest of you will follow.'

'Please, Sire,' began Sir Morvan, a Welsh knight.

'I said we will lead the charge.'

'And I and my men, Sire?' asked Hugh.

'You shall take your stand on our flank, wherever you think you can give us the most help. As for you, Giles, and you, Migbeg, it might be best if you remained here with the princess and Tertius to help guard Merlin. Though if our attack fails there would be little that you could do.'

'That was my thought, Sire,' said Giles. 'By your leave, we will come with you.'

'As you will,' said Arthur. 'And now saddle up and arm yourselves.'

The knights moved off. Brian saddled Gaillard, and picking up his helmet and shield, glanced around for Lianor. She was standing near Merlin's litter watching Tertius who was a little apart from her. When Brian joined her, she signalled him to be quiet and he nodded.

Tertius was looking out to sea where there was—as there was so often in these parts—a thick bank of fog.

This morning it was but a short distance offshore and it was moving slowly down the coast on the northwest wind.

As Brian and Lianor watched, Tertius raised his hands and a strained look came over his face as if he were trying to move or lift something that was too heavy for him. He stood this way for several moments, his face going pale with effort. Then with a sigh, he dropped his hands.

As far as Brian could tell nothing had happened.

'What is he trying to do?' he asked Lianor in a whisper.

'I'm not sure. I think it may have something to do with the fog.'

'But what has that to do with the stones?'

Tertius overheard him. 'There is magic in which you do things,' he said, 'and magic in which you seem to do them. If I am to get the stones to march it, will be in large part an illusion. And to be effective I must bring the fog here. But to do that I must change the direction of the wind.'

'Then it is much the same as it was in England with the weather.'

'It's exactly the same. I know the spell, but I also know that there is no reason why it should work.'

'But spells do work,' said Brian reasonably. 'You made the wind blow during our trip here.'

'I told you I wasn't sure I had done that.'

'Well, Merlin made the rain stop just by saying, "Stop".'

'That was because he was Merlin.'

'And he was your teacher,' said Lianor. 'If he could change the direction of the wind, you can do it too.'

'But I can't,' said Tertius. 'You saw me try.'

'Yes,' said Lianor. 'You were trying much too hard.'
Then, 'Tertius, pick one of those gentians.'

'What?'

'You said Merlin could make the stones march as
easily as he could pick one of those gentians. I want you
to pick one.'

Tertius looked at her for a moment, then he bent
and picked one of the small blue gentians. He placed it
at the base of one of the standing stones and then turned
to the west again. Again he raised his hands, but this time
his face was calm, relaxed. He said something under his
breath and almost at once Brian felt a puff of wind on
his face coming, not from the northwest, but from the
west. The breeze freshened until it was blowing strongly
and the fog began rolling toward them.

Tertius turned back to Lianor.

'No wonder the White Lady and Brian both love you,'
he said.

'I knew you could do it,' she said. 'I will stay with you
for the rest.'

'I had better go,' said Brian.

'Wait,' she said.

She stepped close to him, lifting her face, her eyes wide
and dark. He took her in his arms, holding her close and
kissed her.

'I will not tell you to come back this time,' she whispered. 'I know you will.'

He nodded, kissed her again, then swung up on to
Gaillard and went cantering off along the column of
mounted knights to where the king waited with Sir
Constantine at his side.

'Ah, Brian,' said Arthur. 'I was about to send for you.
How goes it with our young friend?'

'Well, I think, Sire.'

'Good. As things stand now, we can use some help.'

Brian looked down the long hill and his heart sank. For though he had known that the Mongols far outnumbered them, now that they were no longer scattered but were arrayed for battle, their strength looked overwhelming. They sat their shaggy ponies in close packed ranks that filled the entire valley.

'One can say many things about Urlik,' he observed ruefully, 'but he is not niggardly. He has spread us a feast here from which none should go hungry.'

Arthur smiled. 'This is your first battle?'

'Yes, Sire.'

'You will acquit yourself well. How much more time does Tertius require?'

'I do not know, Sire.'

'Well, we will give him as much of it as we can.' And he sat back in his saddle, waiting.

Brian glanced around. Sir Constantine was on the other side of the king, holding Arthur's banner high. Behind them, extending far back down the avenue of stones, were the king's knights, their shields on their left arms. By Arthur's orders they were not carrying lances for this was a battle in which they would be of little use. On Sir Constantine's left was Giles, leaning on his club. On Brian's right was Migbeg, his flint-headed spear in his hand. And beyond him were Hugh, Hob and Wat, their bows braced and with scores of arrows thrust point down in the turf before them.

Now the Mongol ranks opened up and two horsemen rode out in front of them. They were too far away to see clearly but one of them was all in black and rode a black horse. Brian was sure that he was Urlik and he suspected that the other must be the general that they had seen in Nimue's mirror.

'Is that Urlik?' asked Arthur.

'I think so, Sire,' said Brian.

'Mark where he goes. I would like to meet him.'

'By your leave, Sire.' said Hugh, 'I will mark him for you.'

Arthur measured the distance to the two mounted figures far below them, then looked at Hugh.

'You could reach him from here?'

'I can try.'

'We have naught to lose but an arrow. Try then.'

Plucking a blade of grass, Hugh tossed it in the air to gauge the strength and direction of the wind. It was coming from directly behind them, still blowing strongly. Nocking an arrow, he drew, sighted and then raised the point by a fistmele and loosed. The arrow flew upwards, gleaming in the sun, then began to fall in a long arc. Brian held his breath for it was flying straight and true toward Urlik. But glancing up, Urlik raised his hand and at the last moment the arrow veered to the right and buried itself in the turf.

'Well shot, Hugh,' said the king. 'But it seems we must fight, not only Mongols but magic too.'

Scowling, Hugh pulled another arrow from the ground in front of him.

'Let us see if he can turn, not one, but three. Hob, Wat . . .'

His two companions nocked, drew, held and then all three loosed together. Now there were three arrows rising and then falling in a curving path toward the distant figure. Again at the last moment Urlik raised his hand and again the arrows flirted to the side and buried themselves harmlessly in the turf.

'Ah, well,' said Arthur. 'Let us hope he cannot turn

swords as easily as he can a clothyard shaft.' He drew his great sword, Excalibur. 'Think you we can go now?'

Brian turned in his saddle and looked behind him. The fog was moving along the avenue of standing stones now and had almost reached Tertius and Lianor. Catching his glance, Tertius pointed to the fog and then held up his hand.

'In just a moment, Sire,' said Brian. 'When the fog reaches us.' And he drew Starflame.

'That is a noble blade,' said the king' 'Where did you get it?'

'From a Norseman's grave mound,' said Brian. 'It has served me well.'

'Sire,' said Sir Constantine in a strange voice. 'Look!'

Arthur and Brian looked towards him and beyond him and both stiffened. Giles, as tall as the standing stones, had grown impatient with the delay and had moved a few paces forward. And as the fog reached them and rolled over them, the stones seemed to move also, advancing slowly and ponderously behind the frowning giant, then pausing again when he did. But that was not all. Standing in ordered ranks among the stones was a company of short, swarthy warriors wearing Roman helmets and carrying oblong curved shields and heavy hafted spears. Arthur and Brian exchanged glances, then both looked to the right where Migbeg stood. Here the stones seemed to be moving forward also and standing among them were tall, long-haired men armed with bronze swords and bronze pointed spears and others wearing skins and carrying polished stone axes and flint tipped spears like Migbeg's and still others, more apelike with crude wooden clubs.

The fog swirled around them so that they could be seen only dimly. But though the fog was still moving, they were not; they all stood in their places, poised but still, as if waiting for a signal.

'It seems we are to have magic on our side too,' said Arthur.

He glanced back at his knights who seemed little more substantial in the grey mist than the shapes that surrounded them, then he touched his charger with his heels and began the advance.

They went at a slow walk down the long slope at first; the king in the van with Brian at his right and Sir Constantine on his left, the dragon standard floating over their heads. And as they moved forward the whole strange company moved with them; Giles striding along brandishing his club with the massive shapes following him like an army of stone giants, and on their right and left their other shadowy allies; Romans and men of even earlier ages with their weapons of bronze and stone.

Brian had not been certain that any but those who followed the king could see the spectral shapes that advanced with them. But as they started down the hill there was a stir in the Mongol ranks, a wavering and a drawing back. Urlik had moved to the rear, behind the first line of horsemen, but his general had remained where he was and with a sharp order he steadied his men.

Now Arthur raised Excalibur, brought it down and they began their charge, thundering down the hill toward the waiting army below them. Hugh, Hob and Wat were shooting in earnest now, their arrows arching overhead in an unending stream and this time Urlik's magic was either of no avail or it could not protect his whole army, for everywhere the Mongols were falling from their horses, transfixed by the feathered shafts. Giles had broken into a run, brandishing his club and shouting, and on the other side Migbeg was loping along with his spear ready. And everywhere, seemingly as fleet as the galloping horses, were the other shapes dimly seen in the fog that rolled down the hill with them.

The Mongol general, mustached and burly, still sat his horse in front of his men, his curved sword in his hand. Arthur rode directly at him. The Mongol cut at him and Brian threw up his shield, catching the blow. Before he could strike again, Arthur's charger drove into the shaggy pony and horse and rider went down under the thundering hoofs. Then they were into the thick of the enemy. There were grim faces and flashing swords all about them and for a few moments Brian fought without thinking, fending off blows and returning them, Starflame rising and falling steadily.

Then, a short distance ahead of them, Brian saw Urlik surrounded by his bodyguard. Arthur saw him at the same time and turning his charger he drove toward him as he had at the Mongol general. Brian and Sir Constantine turned and rode knee to knee with him, hewing right and left. But always as they fought their way toward him, Urlik retreated before them; never turning his back but moving sideways, keeping his greenish oblique eyes on the king and always keeping his distance from them.

And now at last the Mongols' numbers began to make itself felt and the charge lost its force until they were no longer driving forward at a canter or even a trot, but moving more and more slowly. And though this was Brian's first battle, he knew that this had been Urlik's plan from the first; to let them drive deep into his host and then, when they were surrounded, to overwhelm them.

Even as Brian realised this and even as they came to a halt and Urlik began to smile with triumph, he heard a strange noise above the clash of steel, the shouts and cries and other sounds of battle; a faint, far-off whistling not unlike that of the wind in a falcon's feathers when it stoops on its prey, but louder, much louder. It seemed to come from behind him, and as he heard it, he saw Urlik look up, his eyes widen and his face go white. Brian and the king turned and looked up also and Brian drew in his breath, staring. For diving down out of the grey mist that shrouded the battlefield were half a dozen strange shapes. They were birdlike, but their wings did not move—they remained stiff and outstretched like those of a soaring eagle—and they were so huge that each of them could have carried several men. Down they came, the wind of their passage rising to a screaming roar, and from the sharp nose of each and from the front of their wings there came rapid flashes of fire.

At the same time, as a silence came over the field of battle, there was another sound, just as outlandish and just as menacing; a loud clanking and pounding. And again from behind the king and his knights there came almost a score of other shapes that were just as strange. They were made of metal and they were huge, each almost as large as a small cottage. And though they were not drawn by horses nor even had wheels, they came racing over the uneven ground far faster than a horse could gallop and they too spat angry fire from long tubes, making a noise like thunder.

The stunned silence held for a moment. Then Urlik whirled his horse and went galloping off. And as he did, the Mongols broke, and all began to flee, crying out in terror.

'Arthur and Britain!' shouted Sir Constantine.

There was an answering shout from the scattered

knights and, following Sir Constantine, they went galloping off into the mist after the panic-stricken foe.

Arthur remained where he was and Brian remained
with him. The king looked up and around, seeking the
strange flying and rumbling, thundering objects. But
they were gone as were the other shapes that had come
down the hill with them in the fog.

'You saw what I saw?' he asked Brian.

'I think so, Sire.'

'I have seen strange sights in my time, but none as
strange as that. What made you of it?'

'Only that the things, whatever they were, fought on
our side or seemed to.'

'So it seemed to me. And so it seemed to Urlik too. Let
us hear what our young friend has to say about it.'

They rode back up the slope toward the avenue of
standing stones. The mist was clearing now, thinned by
the wind and the morning sun and they could see bodies
everywhere. A few of them were knights, but all the rest
were Mongols. Brian looked closely at these last as they
went by them and though many of them had arrows in
them or sword wounds, most seemed to have no wounds
at all.

Lianor and Tertius were waiting at the end of the
avenue of standing stones with Hugh, Hob and Wat.

'You and your men did well, Hugh,' said Arthur.
'There were not many of your arrows that did not find a
mark. But you, Tertius, did even better. I said that it
seemed we were to have magic on our side too, but I
did not think it would be such potent magic.'

'Nor did I, Sire.'

'Then was not what took place your doing?'

'Some of it was, but much of it was not.'

'How could that be?'

'When we first came to this place, Brian said there was power here. And of course there is. I made use of that power when I brought the fog here and made the stones seem to walk. But in doing so I must, in some way, have opened a door. For it was not only the stones that marched behind your banner, but all those who had ever fought here. Whether they were real or only shadows like the stones, I cannot say.'

'They seemed real enough to our enemies,' said Arthur, 'even real enough to kill. But while I can understand that there is something else I cannot understand. What were those things like birds that flew overhead and those other metal ones that went without wheels?'

'Do you remember the rest of the prophesy that we reported to you? It was that Urlik's army would be defeated when the stones marched behind your banner and the past and the future became one.'

'Yes,' said Arthur. 'And I suppose those shapes we saw—the Romans and those who carried clubs and weapons of stone and bronze were the past, but . . . Do you mean those other things came from the future?'

'Yes, Sire,' said Tertius. 'Many hundred years from now there will be a great war—a far greater one than has ever been fought before. Britain will again be sore beset. But after having been driven from France with heavy losses, men of Britain and their friends from far across the sea will return here and one of the most important battles of that war will be fought in these parts.'

Arthur frowned. 'But how can that be? I can see how that which was here once could still be here in some shape or form, even as ghosts or memories. But how can that which will only be in time to come be here now?'

'There will be some, in those days to come, who will say that time is not what we think it is.'

'And that is how men will fight then—with weapons such as those?'

'Yes, Sire.'

'Then I am glad that I will not be here to see it. I shall be long gone by then and forgotten.'

'Gone perhaps—though there will be those who will insist that you do but sleep in some hidden place and will return. But you will certainly not be forgotten.'

'But why? There have been many kings before me and I hope there will be many after me.'

'There will be, Sire. But you will be remembered above all others. For you are Arthur. And for as long as Britain lives, you will live too.'

I O

Arthur was still looking thoughtfully at Tertius when Sir Constantine came back with the knights who had followed him.

'You were right about their ponies, Sire,' he said. 'They may be no match for our chargers in battle, but most of them escaped eastward.'

'And Urlik?'

'When we last saw him he was riding back down the coast with his bodyguard.'

'To the castle,' said Brian.

'Probably,' said Arthur. 'We will go after him. I doubt that we can overtake him before he reaches it, but perhaps we can pen him up there.' He hesitated. 'But we have lost at least a score of knights. I do not like to leave them without proper burial.'

'We will tend your dead, Your Majesty,' said a grave voice behind him.

They all turned. Venantius and more than a dozen Druids, all in their long white robes, stood there.

'Greetings, Venantius,' said Tertius. And he made him known to the king.

'You saw the battle?' asked Arthur.

'The end of it,' said Venantius. 'And from what

happened we thought that the spell had been broken and Merlin was himself again. But I see that is not so.'

'No,' said Arthur. 'It was our young friend here who worked the magic that gave us the victory.'

'If Merlin is still under Urlik's spell and Urlik himself has escaped, then it was no victory. You have merely won a battle.'

'So I think too,' said Arthur. 'And that is why we would go after him. If you will see to our dead, we will go now.'

'Go then and go quickly.' And, as he had before, Venantius raised his hands and blessed them.

This time there was no need for anyone to ride double for many of the Mongol ponies and most of the slain knights' horses had remained on the battlefield close to their dead masters. The three outlaws and Migbeg each caught a mount and with Giles leading the two horses that carried Merlin's litter they set off back down the coast.

They reached the open rolling country where they had met Arthur late in the afternoon. As they were about to go west through the woods to the coast they again saw horsemen riding towards them from the south and a short while later Sir Owaine cantered up to them followed by a dozen knights and a company of mounted men-at-arms, the vanguard of Arthur's army.

'God be thanked that you are unharmed, Sire,' he said. 'But I did not think to find you here. Did you not ride on as you planned?'

'We did and fought a great battle and have returned,' said Arthur and he told him what happened.

'If Urlik is indeed in his stronghold, then we have him like a fox in his earth,' said Sir Owaine.

'I think he may prove to be more like a bear than a

fox,' said Arthur. 'One of the great bears of the north who is more dangerous when he is attacked in his den than at any other time. But we shall see.'

One of the men-at-arms was sent back to the Duke of Cornwall to tell him where they were going and they rode through the woods to the coast. When they reached the castle the drawbridge was up and the walls fully manned.

'Well, bear or fox he will not be easy to come at,' said Sir Owaine looking at the castle and the great rock on which it was set.

'It is as strong a fortress as I have ever seen,' said Arthur. 'I do not think it can be taken by assault.'

'What cannot be tossed off at a draught can be drunk in sips,' said Sir Owaine.

'A siege,' said Arthur. 'If Urlik has been foresighted and they are well provisioned, it will not be taken quickly. Still it may be the only way. Let us study it more closely and when Cador gets here we will counsel together.'

Sir Owaine placed the men-at-arms about the castle, just beyond bowshot of the walls. Then Brian led him and the king on a tour of inspection, telling them what he knew about it. When the Duke of Cornwall arrived with the main body of Arthur's forces, they were placed about the castle too, ringing it completely on its landward side. Camp was set up and shortly before dusk Brian, Lianor and Tertius joined the king, the duke, Sir Owaine and Sir Constantine in the royal pavilion.

Sir Owaine was just beginning to outline his plan for the siege when there were heavy running footsteps outside the pavilion and Giles came bursting in.

'Forgive me, Sire,' he said, 'but it's Merlin. He's awake!'

'You're sure?'

'Yes, Sire. He not only moved. He spoke to me.'

'If that is so then this is a day we should all remember! Let us go to him.'

The council broke up as they all hurried out of the pavilion and into the smaller tent near it into which Merlin's litter had been put. He was still lying on it but his eyes were no longer blank and when they came in he turned his head and looked at them.

'Merlin! said Arthur happily. 'It's true then. You are awake.'

'Of course I am,' said Merlin in a hoarse and somewhat strained voice. 'Will you tell this overgrown booby to release me?'

'I'm sorry, master,' said Giles. 'I was so startled when you spoke to me that I could think of nothing but telling the king.' And bending down he untied the strips of cloth that held Merlin to the litter.

With an effort, Merlin sat up.

'Let me help you,' said Tertius. He and Arthur raised the enchanter to his feet. 'You are all right then?'

'Stop asking stupid questions! Of course I'm all right!'

'How were you able to break the spell?'

'No spell lasts forever. I have been struggling against it since it was put on me. Where is Urlik?'

'In his castle,' said Arthur. 'We have him besieged. It will take time but in the end we will have him.'

'It will not take time,' said Merlin. 'You and Tertius come with me.'

And he led the way out of the tent, moving stiffly and a little awkwardly as if he were learning to walk again.

For a moment Arthur and Tertius hesitated, but Merlin had spoken with such authority that neither of them dared question him further and they followed him with the others at their heels. Migbeg was waiting outside and spear in hand, he came with them. They crossed the open ground in silence with all those in Arthur's army and on the castle walls watching them. When they reached the edge of the cliff opposite the gatehouse, Merlin raised his hand and the drawbridge came rattling down. Merlin stepped on to it with the king and Tertius close behind him. But when Brian, Lianor and Migbeg followed, he stopped.

'Hold,' he said, still in the same, strange voice. 'I said the king and Tertius were to come with me. The rest of you remain here.'

'No,' said Brian.

'You dare say no to me?'

'Yes,' said Brian stubbornly. 'Since we brought you Blaise's message about Urlik and then brought you here, it is only right that we should be with you when you face him. Besides I do not think the king should go in there unguarded.'

Now it was Merlin who hesitated. Then,

'Very well,' he said and went on.

'I will come too,' said Sir Owaine.

'And I,' said Sir Constantine.

But as they tried to step on to the drawbridge they staggered back as if they had run into an invisible wall or barrier. With surprised and anxious looks they tried again and again to get through, but whatever it was that had stopped them held firm.

Brian and Lianor looked back at them uneasily, exchanged glances, and then with Migbeg hurried on after Merlin, Arthur and Tertius.

Still walking jerkily as if his joints were stiff, Merlin went through the gatehouse and into the inner bailey. Men-at-arms standing about the bailey and on the walls watched them go. Behind him, Brian heard the port-cullis come rattling down and the drawbridge being raised, but Merlin did not pause or even turn his head. Crossing the bailey, he went straight to the tower keep and through the open door into the great hall. Men-at-arms stood about the walls here too.   Now Merlin stopped, facing the dais at its far end.

Urlik, wearing a dark metal crown, sat on the iron throne with Nimue standing behind him. Blaise, his eyes blank and his face as expressionless as it had been when they saw him in the tower room, sat on the throne to his left. The throne to his right was empty.

'Welcome, Merlin,' said Urlik. 'Come and take your place.'

Like a sleepwalker, Merlin went to the dais and sat down in the throne on Urlik's right. And when he was seated, he became as rigid and as expressionless as Blaise, staring straight ahead of him.

Migbeg hissed softly beside him but Brian did not look at him. He looked at Urlik. And he knew now—as he knew the others knew—that Merlin was still under Urlik's spell: that he had been all this time and that he had led them into a trap.

I I

'So we meet at last, Your Majesty,' said Urlik. Though he gave the king his proper title his smile made it clear that he was mocking him.

'We could have met before this,' said Arthur. 'At Kerrec. It is not my fault that we did not.'

'During the battle, you mean? You should have known that it would not be my way to exchange handstrokes with you.'

'No. Your way is the way of trickery, dark plots and even darker magic.'

'My way is any way that will get me what I want. Though you were not averse to using magic yourself.'

'In a desperate hour, outnumbered and with the lives of my companions at stake. Yes. I permitted it to be used. But it was not black magic.'

'No, it was not. It took me by surprise—as it did my men. Now I think I know what happened and how it was done. But we will talk of that later.' He was looking at Tertius, not the king, when he said this.

Tertius returned his look, saying nothing and again Urlik smiled, a thin, cruel smile.

'You are thinking that you will tell me nothing, but I assure you that you will. You will tell me everything that I wish to know.'

'Do not threaten Tertius or any who are with me, Urlik,' said Arthur. 'It is we who should talk.'

'That was my purpose in bringing you here, Your Majesty,' said Urlik. 'Say on.'

'You have tricked us again and this time you have trapped us. For you now hold me and my friends hostage. But I would point out to you that your plight now is as serious as ours was at Kerrec. Your army is broken and in flight and mine surrounds this castle. My commanders and my men will not leave—not if they must maintain their siege for years—until I and my friends are permitted to leave here unharmed.'

Once again Urlik smiled. 'You think my army has been routed? Show them, Nimue.'

The magic mirror that they had last seen in the conjuring room above now stood at the back of the dais near the throne in which Merlin sat. Going over to it, Nimue passed her hands in front of it and it became bright and clear and in its depths tiny figures appeared; Mongol horsemen. There were only a dozen or more at first but their leader carried a black and red banner which he waved as a signal and soon several score more horsemen joined him and then more and more until there were several hundred of them gathered round him. The captain gave an order and scouts rode off in all directions, clearly to round up the rest of the scattered army.

'Is what we see there to be believed?' Arthur asked Tertius.

'Yes, Sire,' said Tertius. 'The mirror does not lie. It can only show what is.'

'And that you have seen,' said Urlik. 'As your young friend knows, the mirror can also be used to send messages. This I have done. My captains are rallying my forces. It will take them perhaps one more day to gather them together and another to ride here. Then it is your army which will be trapped, surrounded and caught between my horsemen and the castle.'

Arthur looked at him thoughtfully, then nodded.

'Very well. You said that you had brought me here so that we could talk. Say what is in your mind.'

'I think you know, Arthur,' said Urlik. And the king stiffened at being addressed this way. 'Certainly your friends here know, for they have talked to Venantius the Druid and I am sure he told them. For reasons which he understands and perhaps you do too, I mean to have Britain and I will have it. Your life is in my hands now as your kingdom will be when I choose to take it. But I offer them both to you.'

'My life and my kingdom?'

'Your life, the lives of your friends here and those of your men outside my walls. If you will bend your knee and swear allegiance to me, you and all those with you shall go free and you shall continue to rule Britain as my vice-regent.'

Arthur continued to look at him.

'If you know all that you claim to know, Urlik, surely you know what my answer will be.'

'You refuse?'

'Of course. I have been close to death many times. And while I do not welcome it, I do not fear it. Through no choice of mine I have been given a role to play; a role which it seems means a great deal to Britain. I will not betray that role. Nothing can make me betray it.'

'If you bend your knee to me none would know it save your friends here. And they can be sworn to secrecy. Or, if you do not feel they can be trusted, they can be silenced.'

116

'I trust them with my life. As for the rest, you say that none would know it, but that is not true. I would know it. And because I knew it, all would know it.'

Urlik's green eyes became colder and more dangerous. 'I can make you do it.'

Smiling sadly, Arthur shook his head.

'No, Urlik,' he said. 'If you had been able to do it by your dark arts, you would have. But though your magic is strong—strong enough to have robbed me of Merlin— it cannot make me do that which I will not do.'

'How do you know that?'

'I don't know, but I do. You can kill me, but you cannot use me if I do not choose to be used.'

Urlik's eyes now went to Tertius, and Tertius shook his head.

'No,' he said. 'I did not tell him. I did not need to tell him.'

A moment longer Urlik looked at Arthur, studying him. Finally,

'So be it. Then you will die.'

'That may be,' said Arthur, drawing Excalibur. 'But I will not die alone.'

As he drew Excalibur, Brian drew Starflame and moved closer to him so that they were standing side by side, bared blades in hand, waiting.

'You fools!' said Urlik. He gestured and both swords clattered to the stone floor, ripped from their hands by some invisible force. 'I said you will die, Arthur, and you will. But not here and now. For if you did, who would know it? You will die on the castle wall in full sight of your army. And you will die—not now when it is almost dark—but at dawn tomorrow so that all may witness your death.'

He rose from the iron throne and now for the first time, Nimue spoke.

'Is it safe to leave them here, master?' she asked. 'That one,' and she nodded towards Tertius, 'has strange powers. You saw what he could do at Kerrec.'

'He took me by surprise then as I did Merlin,' said Urlik. 'He will not do so again. They will not leave this room. Besides, they will not be alone. For their two friends will remain here also and keep watch over them.'

Nimue glanced at Merlin and Blaise.

'Very well, master,' she said.

Urlik stepped down off the dais and she followed him across the great hall to the door. The men-at-arms that stood about the walls filed out after them and the last one closed the heavy door and they heard the rasp of the bolt as he locked it.

As soon as the door shut, Migbeg picked up Excalibur and Starflame, handed them to Arthur and Brian and then started toward the lancet window behind the iron throne. When he was two or three feet from the dais he jerked upright and staggered back as Sir Owaine and Sir Constantine had when they had tried to follow the king onto the drawbridge. Frowning, he thrust his spear ahead of him. Though there was nothing to be seen the spear stopped dead in midair as if it had struck a stone wall. Turning, Migbeg shrugged.

Brian, Lianor and Arthur each went in a different direction, moving carefully with their hands in front of them. When Brian was a few feet from the door his fingers struck something smooth but unyielding. He ran his fingers down it to the floor then up again as high as he could reach. Looking around, he saw that Lianor and Arthur had been stopped also. They were imprisoned in the centre of the great hall as in a cell by an invisible wall that made a circle about them some twenty or thirty feet across.

'This is why he said we would not leave here,' said Arthur. He walked back toward Tertius who had remained where he was. 'Can you do aught about it?'

'No, Sire,' said Tertius. 'It is one of the most potent of binding spells. Merlin talked of it but never taught me how to do it or undo it.'

'And if he had,' said Arthur glancing at the dais where Merlin and Blaise sat stiffly with blank, staring eyes, 'and if you tried to use it, they would warn Urlik. Thus can the dark arts turn friends into enemies.' He sighed. 'I'm sorry I led you into this trap.'

'You did not lead us into it, Sire,' said Brian. 'We came here by our own choice. And I would not be anywhere else.'

'Nor I,' said Lianor. And both Tertius and Migbeg nodded.

'He understands what we are saying?' asked Arthur looking at Migbeg.

'He cannot or will not speak our tongue, Sire,' said Lianor. 'But he understands everything.'

'There are things that are more important than a common tongue,' said Arthur. He turned again to Tertius. 'When we were at Kerrec you spoke of prophesies made by the White Lady. The one she made about the stones was a true one. Did she say anything else that might be of help to us now?'

'Yes,' said Tertius.

'She said that Urlik could not be killed by anything on earth or of the earth,' said Brian.

'I was not thinking of that one but of the answer to the question you asked, Lianor,' said Tertius.

'How the spell on Merlin could be broken?'

'Yes.'

'What did she say?' asked Arthur.

'That it could be broken by making the journey to the place to which none go willingly and from which few return unchanged,' said Lianor. 'Do you think she meant the castle here?'

'No,' said Tertius. 'But the journey can be made from here as it can be made from anywhere.'

'How?' asked Brian. 'We can't leave here.'

'Our bodies cannot,' said Tertius. 'But it is still possible to go there. Do you remember what Venantius said about Urlik? That he was a shaman, a traveller in the world of darkness.'

'Yes,' said Brian. 'And I didn't know what that meant. Where is this world of darkness?'

'Nowhere and everywhere, mostly within ourselves. It's the far and sometimes frightening country to which we go in our dreams.'

Migbeg nodded, pointed to Merlin and then drew his hand up from his chest as he had when they had talked about Merlin on the ship.

'*He* seems to understand,' said Arthur.

'I think he does,' said Tertius. 'He said Merlin's soul had been stolen from him. And in a sense, he is right. Merlin's body is here. But that which made him Merlin has been taken to that world of darkness that Venantius called Annwn.'

'And you know how to go there?' asked Brian.

'I think so,' said Tertius. 'I'm not sure I could go there myself, but I think I could send someone else there.'

'Very well,' said Brian. 'Send me.'

'Brian, no!' said Lianor.

'It's the reason we came here to France,' said Brian. 'And if it will help us now, I will go.'

Stepping forward, Migbeg tapped himself on the chest.

'He means he will go with you,' said Lianor. 'Do you know how, Migbeg?'

Migbeg nodded and handed her his spear. Taking a small clay pot of blue pigment from the pouch on his belt he dipped a finger in it and drew two lines across his forehead and others down his cheeks and around his eyes. Then putting the blue paint away and loosening his belt, he began a strange dance, turning slowly and stamping first with his right foot and then with his left and at the same time moving in a large circle around them.

'I'm not sure I like this,' said Arthur uneasily. 'It looks heathenish to me.'

'It depends on what you mean by heathen,' said Tertius. 'It's the way the shamans of many people, especially in the north, put themselves into a trance.'

'Must I do it too?' asked Brian.

'No,' said Tertius. 'I don't think it would work with you.'

'What must I do then?'

'Kneel down here.'

Brian knelt and Tertius knelt opposite him.

'Now look into my eyes—deep into them—and make your mind blank. Think of nothing.'

Brian tried to do as he was told, but it was difficult. He found himself thinking about the place to which he was going—if he went—and what it would be like. And when he put that thought out of his mind, others came welling up like water in a forest spring. And all the time he was aware of what was going on around him. He could not see the king or Lianor but he knew that they were standing behind him, watching anxiously, and he could hear the stamping of Migbeg's feet as he continued his dance, head thrown back and eyes half closed, turning and circling about them.

'No,' said Tertius. 'You're thinking about not thinking, but you're still thinking. Look without seeing, as if your eyes were closed. Try to hear nothing, feel nothing as you do in the moment before you fall asleep.'

Again Brian tried, looking—not at Tertius' face—but deep into his eyes. They were dark and serious and Brian felt his own eyes starting to close. Tertius passed his hand in front of them once, twice, and then Brian was looking through and beyond his friend's eyes. Or was he looking into himself? For he was seeing himself lying on his pallet in the tower room at Caercorbin and from the wave of grief, the sense of loss that came over him, he knew that this was the moment, years before, when he had finally believed that his father was dead and would never return from the Holy Land. Then the scene changed. It was later, a little over a year ago, and he was facing the Black Knight, faceless and terrible, in the square at Meliot and what he felt was fear.

His muscles tensed and he tried to draw back, turn away.

'No,' said Tertius, his voice coming from far off. 'Don't do that, Give yourself to it.'

With a great effort Brian made himself relax and go on looking. And now what he saw—but as if from outside himself and high above—was the great hall as it was at that moment; dim, vast and shadowy, lit by a few flaring torches. Merlin and Blaise sat on their thrones on the dais, rigid and silent, and he knelt in the centre of the stone floor staring into Tertius' eyes with Arthur and Lianor watching. Migbeg was the only one who was moving, circling about them and turning faster and faster in what was clearly the climax of his dance. And now, suddenly, a small dark hole appeared in the floor between him and Migbeg. It grew larger and larger, spinning like a whirlpool. Just as it reached Migbeg he shouted loudly and grasped Brian's hand. Then he fell into the whirling, spinning void, pulling Brian after him. And as Brian began to fall, he felt his other hand seized and held. Then the great hall, everything, vanished and there was nothing but darkness.

12

Brian was lying on what seemed to be sand. He sat up. Migbeg, stretched out next to him, was just sitting up also. He smiled at Brian and they both got to their feet. Then, looking past Brian, he smiled even more broadly. Brian turned.

'Oh, no,' he said. For there, brushing the sand from her tunic, was Lianor.

'Why are you looking so surprised?' she asked.

'I suppose I shouldn't be,' he said. 'I felt someone take my hand just as I started falling and I should have known it was you.'

'Of course,' she said. 'I wasn't sure it would bring me here but I thought it was worth trying.'

'And what if, instead of bringing you here, it had kept me from going?'

'It didn't. Anyway I'm here and there's no way to send me back so you might as well make the best of it.'

'I suppose I'll have to.' Despite his misgivings he could not help smiling too. 'I see you brought Migbeg's spear.'

'Oh. Yes.' It was lying at her feet where she had dropped it and she picked it up and gave it to Migbeg. He nodded his thanks and they looked around.

They were in the strangest place Brian had ever seen;

a sandy waste that extended as far as he could see in every direction. For a moment he was not sure why it seemed so strange, then he realized there were several reasons.

First, there was the light. It was dim, so dim that the three of them cast no shadows, and it seemed to have no source. For when he looked up he saw that there was no sun or moon or even any sky above them, only a faintly luminous greyness.

Second, there was the waste itself. The sand, fine and red in some places and yellow in others, was in constant motion; not shifting as sand does when blown by the wind, but rising and falling gently like the sea on a calm day.

'What did Tertius call this place?' asked Brian.

'It was Venantius who gave it a name,' said Lianor. 'He called it Annwn.'

'But they both said it was a world of darkness.'

'Well, you cannot call it a world of light. And there may be parts that are darker than this.'

'That's true. Which way do you think we should go?'

'I don't think it matters. If we are meant to find Merlin we will find him no matter which way he go.'

'Still we've got to go in one direction or another,' said Brian logically. 'Migbeg, you decide.'

Shrugging, Migbeg tossed his spear into the air. It fell with its flint head pointing somewhat to their right.

'That way then?'

'It's as good as any.'

And so they set off, going where the spear pointed. Walking was not easy for though they did not sink into the coloured sand its constant motion made their footing uncertain, and when they looked back they saw that the sand's slow heaving had erased their footprints.

It occurred to Brian that with no sun or moon to give them their direction and no footprints to follow it would be difficult to find their way back. But he did not say anything about this.

Suddenly, far ahead, two very odd creatures appeared and came toward them. They seemed to be some sort of bird but they were like no birds that any of them had ever seen before. They were almost as tall as a man and had long blue legs and short wings. Their bodies were round and covered with fur rather than feathers and their beaks were short and triangular. They looked at the three strangers with wide, surprised eyes and when Lianor spoke to them they squawked and ran off on their stilt-like legs.

They continued on across the sandy waste and abruptly came to the end of it; a place where the sand no longer rose and fell but became firm and solid as a beach. Beyond this rim of sand was a heath that was somewhat rolling, covered with springy turf and dotted with clumps of fern and heather and an occasional rock.

There were some low hills ahead of them and as they drew near them Migbeg began looking around uneasily.

'What's wrong, Migbeg?' asked Brian.

Migbeg shook his head but did not answer.

'For some reason this all looks familiar,' said Brian.

'Like the heath where we first met Migbeg,' said Lianor.

'That's it,' said Brian, remembering. 'But then why is he anxious?'

'He must have his reasons. You remember how the White Lady described this; as the place to which none go willingly.'

'But he did come willingly. It was he who brought us here.'

'Yes. But he didn't know what we would find here and it must remind him of something unpleasant.'

They came to a low ridge, climbed it and when they got to the top Migbeg paused, looking at the hill directly ahead of them. It was barren and rocky and crowning it was one particular rock that was dark and somehow menacing, like a huge brooding face.

Migbeg pointed to it and again shook his head.

'You don't want to go that way' asked Lianor.

He nodded.

'Then we won't,' said Brian.

They went down the ridge and turned to the right, walking away from the hill along the bottom of the valley that lay between it and the ridge. The valley became deeper and narrower until it was little more than a cleft through which they had to go in single file. Migbeg was leading the way and walking quickly as if anxious to get as far as possible from the hill. They came to a place where the rift was so narrow that Migbeg had to turn sideways to squeeze through. Brian and Lianor followed him and found that Migbeg had stopped again and was staring ahead of him, his eyes wide and his face drawn.

They were in a valley that was perhaps a quarter of a mile across, a cup in the hills with steep, almost vertical walls. And though the rift through which they had approached it had seemed to be straight, it must have curved to the left for there, opposite them, was the hill with the huge, face-like rock near its top that they had been trying to avoid.

'Migbeg, why does this place frighten you so?' asked Brian.

Migbeg did not answer.

'You know we're your friends,' said Lianor. 'Tell us.'

Reluctantly Migbeg turned to her, pointed to himself and held his hand out at about shoulder height.

'Years ago, when you were younger—about sixteen years old,' said Lianor, translating his sign language.

He nodded and went on, continuing to make his stylized gestures which she interpreted.

'You went out or were sent out alone, as is the custom among your people. You had no weapons or food. It must have been a kind of test or initiation,' she explained in an aside to Brian.

Again Migbeg nodded, then pointed upwards, held up three fingers and made a sweeping gesture that took in the valley.

'After three days you came here. And then what? What happened?'

Once more he shook his head, and it was clear that he was going to say no more.

'We know that he's a brave man,' said Brian. 'So whatever happened here must have been very bad. All right, Migbeg. We'll go back.'

He turned towards the opening through which they had just come—and it wasn't there! Somehow the cleft had closed and behind them was a rock wall as solid and sheer as the sides of the valley.

Brian and Lianor exchanged thoughtful glances.

'Look, Migbeg,' said Brian, 'what happened years ago didn't happen here. It happened in a place that looks like this. Now we seem to be trapped. We can't go back and the only way out of this valley is there.' He pointed to an opening on its far side. 'Will you go there with us?' Migbeg hesitated, then nodded.

'Good,' said Brian.

They spread out with Brian on one side of Migbeg and Lianor on the other and started across the valley. As they did, what little light there was faded and it became darker, so dark that they could barely see the surrounding walls of the valley.

Though the floor of the valley was level, it was stony and they had to pick their way across it carefully. They were about half way across, walking slowly, when there was a sudden wailing call off to their left. Migbeg froze, clutching his spear. The call was answered by another to their right and still others ahead and behind him. Then, as Migbeg looked around wildly, a dozen or more weird shapes appeared out of the half darkness and came toward them.

Though they walked on two legs, they were not men for they were taller than men, their bodies were hairy and their heads were those of beasts or creatures in a nightmare; some wolflike, some like birds of prey and one with branching horns like that of a stag.

Moving lightly and quickly they came towards the three and now Brian could see that their hands were talons with sharp, curving nails.

With a moan, Migbeg sank to the ground, covering his face. Brian drew Starflame and Lianor her dagger and with Migbeg between them they prepared to fight the monsters off.

Weaving back and forth, almost dancing, the creature closed in, teeth and claws gleaming. They ignored Brian and Lianor and tried to get at Migbeg. The one with the horns seemed to be their leader. It gestured and one with a wolf's head darted in. Brian cut at it, but it ducked under his blow and raked Migbeg's chest with its talons. Migbeg cried out in terror and pain and blood welled up from the gashes. Again Brian slashed at it and though this time his blow was true and caught it on the neck, its flesh offered no resistance. The blade passed through it, and the monster drew back unharmed.

Now another darted in and another, dodging Brian's sword and taking no hurt when he did reach them. Behind him he could hear Lianor panting as she slashed at the demonic shapes with her dagger. Then,

'Migbeg,' she cried. 'You must help us. Do you hear? You must help us!'

A moment longer he crouched there, his body and arms gashed and red with blood. Then, with a shout, he leaped to his feet and hurled his spear at the horned monster. It staggered back with the spear in its chest. Then it and all the other nightmare figures disappeared.

Brian and Lianor looked about them.

'Were they real?' asked Brian.

'They seemed to be,' said Lianor, 'even though we could not hurt them. When they clawed Migbeg, he bled.'

But when they looked at Migbeg the blood was gone and there were no wounds on his body, only the faint marks of old scars.

Migbeg was looking about also. Picking up his spear, he examined the flint point. There was no blood there either. Then, coming back, he embraced Lianor and Brian gratefully.

'There's no need for that,' said Lianor. 'You did it yourself. But I don't think that that particular night-mare—if that's what it was—will trouble you again.'

Gravely Migbeg nodded.

13

They continued on across the level floor of the valley.

Though the light remained dim they found the opening on the far side with no difficulty and started through it. The earth underfoot was hardpacked and firm but all at once it seemed to become stone and their footsteps began echoing as if they were no longer in the open but in an enclosed passage. Then there was light ahead of them and when they approached it they saw that it was a torch set in a bracket on a wall and that they were in a flagged passage.

And now it was Lianor who was looking about her uneasily.

'What is it, Lianor?' asked Brian.

'Don't you recognize this? Don't you know where we are?'

There was an archway just beyond the torch with a stair leading down. Opposite it was a door. Both looked familiar.

'The palace at Meliot,' said Brian. 'That's the door to the solar.'

'Yes,' said Lianor. 'We must go in.'

'Why?'

'Because we must. At least, I must,' and her eyes dark and her face pale and strained she went toward the door.

'Lianor, wait,' said Brian. And as she paused with her hand on the latch, 'Remember what happened with Migbeg. This may seem like Meliot but it's not. It can't be. And whatever happens here or seems to happen will not be real.'

She did not answer but lifted the latch, pushed the door open and went in.

The solar was exactly as he remembered it except that where the king's chair had stood near the window there was now a bed. And in the bed, her eyes closed, was a woman who seemed only a few years older than Lianor and who looked very much like her.

Lianor's father, the king, and her twin sister, Alys, were standing beside the bed. They turned as Lianor came into the room and the woman in the bed opened her eyes.

'Lianor?' she whispered.

'Yes,' said Lianor. She hurried to the bed and knelt beside it. 'Oh, mother . . .'

'Dear child,' said the queen. She raised a thin hand and stroked Lianor's hair. 'I hoped you would come before it was too late.'

'You're not going to die,' said Lianor, her voice choked. 'You're not!'

'I fear there is naught that can be done about it,' said the queen.

Lianor looked up at her father and he turned away.

Brian frowned. As he recalled, the queen had died shortly after Lianor and her sister were born. And if that was true why was this happening and why was Lianor accepting it?

'No, no,' said Lianor. 'I am a good healer. I will save you.'

Smiling sadly, the queen shook her head.

'I am tired,' she said, 'but I waited till you got here.'

Then, 'Is there anything you wish to ask me?'

'Yes,' said Lianor, her head bowed. 'Which of us is the older, Alys or I?'

'Why do you wish to know that?'

'You know why.'

'Yes,' sighed the queen. 'But it does not matter now.'

'It does,' said Alys suddenly. 'Tell her, mother.'

'No.'

'Yes,' said Alys firmly. 'I have told her many times but she would not believe me.'

'Very well,' said the queen. 'Alys is the older by several hours.'

'Oh, no,' moaned Lianor.

'Yes,' said Alys. 'I was born with no difficulty. It was your birth that killed her.'

'No, no,' said Lianor again. She turned to the king. 'Father . . .'

'I'm sorry, Lianor,' he said slowly. 'It's true.'

'But then you must hate me. How you must hate me!'

He shook his head. 'I do not hate you. Though I have tried, I do not love you as much as I do Alys—I cannot. But . . .'

'Father!' called Alys.

The king looked down at his wife. Her eyes had closed and she was still. Bending down, he kissed her on the forehead, then crossed her arms on her breast.

'Mother,' sobbed Lianor. 'Oh, mother . . .'

'Lianor, don't!' said Brian going to the bed. 'Have you forgotten what I said to you outside there? None of this is true.'

'It is,' said Lianor. 'All my life I have tried to deny it, but I always knew it was true. It was I who was responsible for my mother's death.'

'And do you know what you must do about it?' asked Alys.

'Yes,' said Lianor. And getting to her feet she ran from the room.

'Lianor!' said Brian. He started to go after her but the king restrained him.

'Stay Brian,' he said. 'Let her go.'

'Why?'

'Because it will be easier for her. You heard her. She knows what she must do to pay for this.'

'Why must she pay? She has done nothing.'

'She thinks she did. And so she must pay.'

'Pay how?'

'By giving up that which means more to her than anything else.'

Brain stared at the king. 'You mean me?'

'Yes, Brian.'

'She can't do that! I won't let her. I'll find her and tell her so.'

The king smiled a wintery smile. 'Very well, Brian. If you can find her, you may tell her so.

'What do you mean? Where has she gone?'

'You said you would find her. If you do, all may still be as you wish. If not . . .' He shrugged.

'Would you like me to help you, Brian?' asked Alys, smiling provocatively at him.

'No!' he said.

He hurried to the door and went out with Migbeg following him. The corridor was empty but he could hear voices and laughter below and he went down the stairs.

Sir Amory, the king's seneschal, was standing at the entrance to the great hall.

'I am looking for the Princess Lianor,' said Brian. 'Is she here?'

'Yes, Sir Brian.'

Brian looked into the great hall. It was bright with burning tapers and by their light he could see that it was crowded with ladies, all gaily dressed. But all were masked.

'So this what the king meant!'

'Yes, Sir Brian. You may go in and look for her. But you may not remove any of their masks.'

Frowning, Brian went in. As he did, musicians in the gallery began playing and the ladies began to move in a slow pavane.

'Dance with me, Brian,' said one, holding out a white hand to him.

'No, with me,' said another.

'Brian, don't you know me?' asked a third sadly—and all were Lianor's height, carried themselves as she did and spoke with her voice.

'Well, Brian?' said Alys coming up beside him.

'I do not like this game!' he said angrily.

'It is no game,' she said. And somehow he knew that it was true. That what happened here would free Lianor from something that had always haunted her or leave her in thrall to it forever. 'You may take one of us with you, but only one.'

Then, as he hesitated, 'Is is so hard to find the one you love?'

'Brian, you cannot leave me here. You cannot!' whispered a maiden in green and the choke in her voice was like a dagger thrust. Surely this was Lianor. Green was her favourite colour. He reached for her, then paused as Migbeg touched his arm, pointing.

At the far end of the hall, crouched by the hearth of the huge fireplace was a drab figure in grey. He pushed his way through the gracefully swaying figures and saw that it was an old crone in a stained and ragged cloak, just such a cloak as Lianor had worn when she had disguised herself more than a year before and come with him and Tertius on the quest for the Knight with the Red Shield.

'Lianor,' he said.

The old crone lifted her head. Though her hood was pulled forward, shadowing her face, he saw that she wore a mask too.

'Who is Lianor?' she asked in a harsh, cracked voice.

'The lady I love.'

'And you think I am she? Then kiss me.' And she held out her arms to him.

Brian hesitated. It had taken him many weeks to see through Lianor's disguise during that long journey of theirs, but he knew that this was no disguise; this woman's hair was not dyed and the lines and wrinkles on her face were not artfully drawn there but real.

'Still not sure, Brian?' asked Alys who had followed him.

He did not answer but his silence was answer enough.

'Poor Brian,' said Alys mockingly. 'And poor Lianor. Still, it need not be she whom you take with you. Remember that you were in love with me before you were in love with her.'

It was true. It had been Alys whom he had loved first and it had been to win her that he had gone on the quest. And looking at her now—her golden hair and eyes as blue as larkspur—her beauty shook him again as it had the first time he had seen her.

'Why not? she whispered, leaning toward him. 'You chose her instead of me, but now you are free to choose again.'

The music was still playing. She smelled of lavender. He looked again at the old crone who had dropped her arms and was huddled again on the hearth.

'Lianor,' he said pleadingly. 'If you are Lianor give me a sign.'

She did not look up, did not move. And while he could not see her eyes, he saw the two tears that appeared below the edge of her mask and ran slowly down her cheeks. Reaching down, he took her by the arms and lifted her to her feet.

'Remember,' said Alys behind him, 'whoever you choose now it will be for always.'

'I know,' said Brian. And taking the frail, stooped figure in his arms, he kissed her on the mouth. For a moment he held her. Then the body that had seemed so thin and bent became firm, full and strong and the lips warm.

'Brian . . .'

He pushed back her hood and pulled off her mask.

'Oh, Brian,' said Lianor again. And now she was sobbing with deep, racking sobs. He kissed her again, took her in his arms again and held her close.

14

When Brian released her, Lianor was no longer wearing her old cloak but was dressed as she had been; in hose and a tunic. She dried her eyes, glanced at Brian and then at Migbeg who was grinning happily at her.

'Shall we go on?' she asked.

Brian nodded gravely. Alys and the masked figures had disappeared and the great hall was dim and empty. They went past the stair that led up to the solar, opened the outer door of the palace that was usually guarded by two men-at-arms and went out. They were in the town square and that was empty too.

And now, though he was not sure why, Brian found it was his turn to feel uneasy. Was it because Lianor and Migbeg had each been through a terrifying ordeal and it was probable therefore that he would face one too? But if that was so why should he feel anxious here, in the deserted town square?

There was a sound of heavy footsteps, the clink of mail and suddenly Brian knew the answer. Into the square from the narrow street on its far side came two figures; the Black Knight who had been a threat to Meliot for so long and his lean, grey-bearded captain.

They were not mounted as they had been when Brian had last seen them; they were on foot. But the Black

Knight moved with the slow, controlled movements that Brian had found so frightening and wore the black helmet and dinted rusty hauberk he had worn then and carried the same black shield. His captain carried another helmet and shield. They came a few paces into the square and then stopped, blocking the way to the street.

Brian suddenly realized that Lianor and Migbeg were both looking at him.

'Remember what you said to me before,' said Lianor. 'This may seem to be Meliot, but it's not. And whatever seems to happen here will not be real.'

'While we are here it will be real,' said Brian.

'You still need not fight him.'

'We came here to find Merlin and Blaise. The only way out of the square is that way, where they are.' And he started toward the two still figures.

'But, Brian . . .' she began, then paused.

He knew what she had been about to say. How can you fight the Black Knight when, in the end, he turned out to be your father?

That was the question: was this his father? And if he was, was he Sir Owaine as he was now—as proud of Brian as Brian was of him—or was he what he had been when he and Brian had first met; a man whose memory was gone so that he knew no one, not even who he was himself?

Reaching the tall figure, Brian paused.

'Father,' he said.

The Black Knight, faceless in his helmet, did not move.

'Who do you call father?' asked his captain.

'Your master.'

'He is no one's father.'

'Let him speak for himself.'

'He does not speak. I speak for him. What would you with him?'

'If he does not know me, nothing. Only to go by you and leave here in peace.'

'You know the custom—or should. No one leaves here in peace. No one goes by him unless they can overcome him.'

'Father, I beg you to let us by. Do you not know me? I am your son, Brian.'

Still the Black Knight neither moved nor gave any sign that he had either heard or understood.

'Have done,' said the captain. 'He hears nothing, knows nothing save combat. If you do not wish to fight him, then begone.'

'Press me not!' said Brian angrily. 'The choice is still mine.'

'No longer. Get you gone or I will take my blade to you.' And he put his hand to his sword. Without thinking, Brian reached for Starflame.

'Brian!' cried Lianor.

He leaped back and steel flashed, grazing his sleeve. For when he touched the hilt of his sword the Black Knight had drawn and cut at him.

'Fly!' said the captain. 'Once he has drawn I can do nothing with him!'

'No,' said Brian.

'Go, you fool! He'll kill you!'

'No,' said Brian again, drawing Starflame. For, recovering, the Black Knight was advancing on him again.

'Coward!' said Lianor fiercely. 'At least give him time to arm himself!'

'I told you I can do nothing with him,' said the captain. 'But here.' And he threw Brian the shield he was carrying. Brian caught it, slipped his arm through the straps and bareheaded turned to face the helmeted and menacing figure.

For a moment they were still, shields raised and swords raised, studying one another. Then the Black Knight feinted, shifting his weight as if about to move to the left and then moving to the right and striking a great overhand blow at Brian. Brian slid away from it, not even needing to catch it on his shield, but this was a feint also. For without checking his blade, the Black Knight brought it around and struck again at Brian, backhanded. Brian threw up his shield to fend it off and the force of the blow jarred his whole body. He raised Starflame for a counterstroke, then caught himself. For how could he strike when, in spite of the Black Knight's silence, he knew who he was—or who he might be?

As he hesitated, the Black Knight struck again, another great swinging blow followed by a slashing backhanded one. Again Brian warded them off, but this time he did not even raise his sword but only moved sideway to make himself a more difficult target.

The Black Knight followed him, pressing him hard, and cold sweat beaded Brian's forehead. For though he had known, when they had fought here over a year before, that he was facing a skilled and deadly swordsman, he had felt that if he could withstand the Black Knight's initial attack his own youth and strength would begin to tell and he could overcome him. But how could he do so now when he could not fight back?

Then, just as he had known who was coming into the square and what his ordeal was to be, Brian knew what he must do. Though he had done it in ignorance—for he had not known who the Black Knight was—he had raised his sword against his father and must be prepared to pay for it.

Recovering from a thrust that Brian had caught on his shield, the Black Knight lifted his sword for another great stroke—and Brian lowered his sword and shield and bowed his bared head, awaiting it.

He heard Migbeg gasp and Lianor moan. There was a clatter and a clang as the Black Knight dropped his sword and shield and Brian felt himself seized and held in a fierce but tender embrace. Hot tears came into his eyes—tears of love and relief—blinding him.

15

The Black Knight and his captain were gone and Brian, Lianor and Migbeg were alone in the square. Lianor came to him and looked at him anxiously.

He forced a smile.

'We can go now,' he said somewhat huskily. She nodded, her eyes dark and serious, then smiled also.

They left the square by the narrow, cobbled street that went by the inn and the shops of the merchants. The town gate was open and they went through it. There should have been two roads here; the one that climbed the hill and eventually led to Caercorbin and the other that went to the ford at the river where the Black Knight had waited for so long, challenging all who would go that way. But now there was only one; the one that led to the river and the forest beyond, so they took it.

They waded the river and followed the road on the far side into the forest. It was wide and rutted for a short distance, then narrowed to a track and curved to the left. This was where the Black Knight's keep had stood, guarding the route to the east and south. Now, instead of the keep, there was a low, rocky hill. The road went to the base of the hill and ended at an opening that was just a little higher than a tall man.

'There?' asked Brian.

'There does not seem to be any other way,' said Lianor. They paused at the entrance to the cave, peering into the darkness beyond.

'We should have a light,' said Brian.

'We have no fire.'

'No, but . . . He drew Starflame and it did not surprise him that in this place where so much was strange, it should glow with a faint light. Holding it aloft like a torch he led the way into the cave.

It ran straight for a while, the walls smooth and dark on either side of them and the roof arching overhead. Then they came to a fork, one branch going right and one left.

Brian looked inquiringly at Lianor and when she shrugged, he said, 'All right. We'll go left. But we should leave a mark of some kind so we can find our way back.'

They looked around for some pebbles or loose stones that they could leave to show the way they had taken, but there were none. Taking the small pot of blue paint from his pouch, Migbeg dipped his finger into it and made a mark on the wall.

'Good,' said Brian.

They started along the left-hand passage. It dipped down somewhat, turning first right and then left, then forked again; this time into three openings. Here they took the middle one, Migbeg again marking the side of it with his blue paint. On they went, deeper and deeper into the darkness and the silence, through a place where the passage opened into a huge cavern with stalactites glittering overhead like great stone icicles and across a shallow underground stream.

They were deep under the hill now, so deep that they seemed to feel it pressing down on them. The passage branched again and again, still twisting and turning and

144

always Brian took one branch or the other without pausing or thinking and always Migbeg marked the way as if he were blazing a forest trail. Finally the passage narrowed into an archway like a door. They went through it and then stopped.

They were in a small vaulted chamber. On its far side were two thrones like the ones in the great hall of Urlik's stronghold. And sitting on them as stiff and motionless as they had been when they had last seen them were Merlin and Blaise.

They went over to them.

'Merlin, we're here,' said Brian. 'We've come to take you back with us.'

The elderly enchanter did not move. His eyes were blank and empty, seeing nothing.

'Merlin,' said Brian again. He took him by the arm. It was cold and stiff and when he tried to lift him it was like trying to move a statue.

'What are we going to do?' he asked Lianor. 'We came here to bring them back, but we can't. And if we don't, the king will die.'

There is one chance,' said Lianor slowly.

'What's that?'

'The word and sign that Venantius gave me. He was not sure when or how I should use them, but . . .'

'We have nothing to lose. Try it, Lianor.'

'Very well.' She reached for her dagger. Then, remembering, 'He said I was not to use metal. May I have your spear, Migbeg?'

Migbeg gave it to her and with the keen flint head she scratched the sign that was like three rays of sunlight on the stone floor. Then, stepping back, she said the word. It was a strange word, mostly vowels, and it was intoned rather than spoken.

For a moment nothing happened. Then Merlin and Blaise both moved. It was so slight a movement that at first Brian was not sure he had not imagined it. But when he looked closely at Merlin's face it seemed to him that while his eyes were still unfocused, they were no longer blank.

'Merlin,' he said. And now Merlin's head turned and he looked at Brian—without recognition, but apparently seeing him.

'You're free now,' said Brian with an assurance he did not feel. 'Come with us.'

Again he took the enchanter by the arm and wordlessly, his face still without expression, Merlin rose. Lianor and Migbeg were helping Blaise to his feet. Both magicians moved slowly and stiffly, but they did move.

They went out of the small chamber, Brian leading Merlin and holding Starflame high to light the way, followed by Lianor and Migbeg with Blaise between them.

They went up the long passage, guided by the blue marks Migbeg had left on their way in. They crossed the underground stream, went through the cavern and continued on, moving slowly upward through the darkness. There was no way of telling how long they had been in the strange, unreal world and, afraid of what might be happening in Urlik's great hall, Brian did his best to get Merlin to walk more quickly, but it was useless. He continued to move slowly and deliberately, neither looking at Brian nor responding to anything he said.

Finally, even at their maddeningly slow pace, they reached the mouth of the cave. Brian had feared that they would have to retrace their entire journey, going back through Meliot and the valley in the hills and he was not even sure they could find their way. But when they came out of the cave the forest was gone and in its place was the desert with its sand in constant wavelike motion.

They set out across it, supporting the two magicians.

'Have you thought of how we're going to get back?' asked Lianor.

'No,' said Brian. 'You were the one who said that if we were meant to find Merlin and Blaise, we would. I think the same thing is true now. If we are meant to get back, we will.'

'You're learning,' said Lianor with a small smile.

'I've learned a great deal since we've been here,' said Brian. 'I'm still not sure what it all means, but . . .'

He broke off. Far ahead of them was a dark, swaying column. It seemed to be a kind of whirlwind that was moving over the wasteland, drawing the sand upward with its spinning motion. It came toward them and Brian tightened his grip on Merlin's arm. Then it was upon them. Blinded and buffeted, Brian was spun around like a leaf in an eddy. Then his feet left the ground as he was drawn upward.

16

'Brian . . .'

He shut his eyes even more tightly, turned away from the voice and tried to pull his cloak around him for he was cold and tired and didn't want to wake yet. But there was no cloak.

'Brian,' said the voice again, urgently, insistently.

He gave up and opened his eyes. He was lying on the floor of the great hall of Urlik's castle and Tertius was bending over him. He stared at him for a moment then, remembering, sat up.

'Lianor?' he asked. 'Migbeg?'

'They're all right,' said Tertius. 'Here, let me help you.'

He held out his hand and Brian took it and, with some difficulty, got to his feet. For he was not only cold from lying on the stone floor, but stiff as well. Migbeg was already standing and the king was helping Lianor up and putting an arm around her for she was shivering.

'You've been asleep,' said Tertius. 'Or at least you seemed to be. Not just the two of you, but Lianor too.'

'I went with them,' explained Lianor.

'That's what we thought,' said Tertius. 'Though we did not know how you had done it. We did not want to wake you or call you back because we thought you might still be able to do what you set out to do. But . . .'

'But we did!' said Brian. 'We found Merlin and Blaise, freed them and brought them back with us.'

Something in Tertius' face made him break off. He turned and for the first time looked at the dais. By the dim light that came through the lancet window behind it —the first light of a grey, overcast day—he saw Merlin and Blaise sitting on their thrones; sitting as still and stiff as when he had last seen them, their faces expressionless and their eyes blank and staring.

'But we did do it!' he repeated. 'Lianor broke the spell with the word and sign that Venantius gave her.' He turned to her for corroboration and she shook her head.

'I thought so too. But many things happened there— or seemed to happen—that could not have happened.'

'But this wasn't the same. They didn't speak or seem to know us, but they came with us. Perhaps if you did it again now . . .'

'Peace, Brian,' said Arthur gently. 'You did what you could, but there is little time for any more. It is almost dawn. That is why we woke you.'

Brian looked at the window again. It faced west so he could not see the sun, but only the heavy, low-hanging clouds over the sea.

'But it will not take any time. Try it, Lianor. You must try it!'

'Very well,' said Lianor. She held out her hand and once more Migbeg gave her his spear. With its flint point she scratched the three lines on the stone floor and said the word of power. She was still holding the spear when the door opened and Urlik and Nimue came in, followed by a dozen men-at-arms.

149

Going straight to his throne, Urlik sat down between Merlin and Blaise. Nimue took her place behind him and the men-at-arms stationed themselves about the walls. Nimue was in a crimson robe this morning, but Urlik wore the same dark robe he had worn before and his black crown was on his head.

'I trust you rested well, Arthur?' he said.

'Well enough,' said the king quietly.

'Not so well, I hope, that you did not think about the offer I made you.'

'There was no need to think about it. I gave you my answer.'

'And you have not changed your mind?'

'No, Urlik.'

'So be it. Your friends outside the wall grow restive. I quieted them by telling them that you would speak to them. And speak you shall. For I will give you time to say farewell to them before you die.'

'And then?' asked Arthur.

'Need you ask?' They will launch an assault on the castle—which they‚they have not done yet for fear I would injure you. The assault will fail, but it will keep them here until my army arrives, surrounds and destroys them.' Then to the men-at-arms, 'Take him to the wall over the gatehouse.'

Though he knew that it was useless—that Urlik could disarm him with a wave of his hand as he had done before—Brian drew Starflame. And as he did, Merlin and Blaise both moved again; not almost imperceptibly as they had in the underground chamber, but definitely and decisively. Both rose. Merlin brought his hand down in a slashing gesture and a pillar of flame roared up from the stone floor in front of Urlik, blinding him and everyone else in the great hall.

As Brian staggered back, shielding his eyes, someone caught his arm.

'Your sword, Brian,' said a voice he had not heard in some time. 'Quickly!'

It was Merlin who, with Blaise, had hurried down from the dais to join them. Dazed and incredulous, Brian gave him Starflame. Merlin drew a circle around all of them with it and again flames leaped up so that they were surrounded by a ring of fire.

'Then we did bring you back!' said Brian. 'We did free you!'

'Yes,' said Merlin. 'But the spell was a strong one and we were under it for a long time. We had to wait until our powers had returned to us.'

Joyfully Brian embraced him and Merlin patted him on the back, gripped the king's hand and that of Tertius. But he did this all absentmindedly, his face grim and his eyes on the dais.

Looking past the pillar of fire, Brian saw that Urlik had recovered. He gestured and the column of fire vanished and the flames that surrounded them died, leaving only a ring of white light.

Leaning forward on his throne, Urlik looked long and hard at Merlin.

'So you finally broke my spell, Merlin,' he said.

'Not I, Urlik. I had friends who did it.'

Urlik's eyes went to Tertius, then back to Merlin.

'That pupil of yours. Nimue warned me about him.'

'It was not he alone. Others helped.'

'It does not matter. The end will be the same. I overcame you once. Do you think you can stand against me now?'

'You took me by surprise then. We shall see.'

'Yes. We will.'

Urlik jerked his head and Nimue came forward to stand beside him. At the same time Blaise moved over to stand next to Merlin. For several moments they were all still with Merlin's eyes and Urlik's fixed on one another. Though nothing was said or done, Brian could feel the tension as when two champions circle one another, swords ready, each studying the other and searching for an opening.

Suddenly Urlik's hand shot out and from the four corners of the great hall long darts like spears of ice sped towards the group that was huddled within the circle of light. But when Urlik moved, Merlin moved also. He gestured and the ring of light shot upward into a white wall. The spears of ice struck it and were shattered.

Once more all was still for a moment. Then Urlik made a sweeping pass and a shape began to take form in the darkest corner of the great hall. It became larger and larger and as it moved out into the light they could see that it was an enormous serpent, its body thicker than that of a man. Urlik's first attack had come so suddenly and Merlin's response had been so quick that it was all over before Brian had realized what was happening. This time the deliberate movements of the serpent increased Brian's horror. It writhed forward slowly, its dark body gleaming and its jaws agape. Reaching the ring of light, it turned and began moving around it, its forked tongue flickering. Then, when it had encircled the ring and all those within it, its coils tightened, con-tracted—and such was its strength that the ring began to give, become smaller.

Brian reached for Lianor and pulled her close to him. Merlin still held Starflame. He raised it and another sword, like Starflame except that it had a blade of fire, appeared in mid-air outside the ring of light. He brought

Starflame down and the other sword slashed down also, cutting off the serpent's head. It reared up, its body jerking spasmodically, then it disappeared and the ring of light regained its original shape.

Again Urlik remained still for a moment. Then his hand shot out and up. And this time the shape that appeared materialized out of the darkness over their head, *inside* the ring of light. Like the serpent, it was huge. It was not a bird for its wings were leathery, batlike. It had a long neck and its open mouth was armed with several rows of sharp teeth. It came diving down at them from the rooftree of the great hall with such speed that Brian barely had time to tighten his arm around Lianor.

But quick as Urlik had been, Merlin was quicker. He raised Starflame, pointing, and from the very centre of the magic ring a tree shot up. It was a white tree—a tree of light. Its branches extended over all their heads, sheltering them, and each branch was armed with long, gleaming thorns. The winged monster crashed into the tree, the thorns piercing its body in a dozen places. It screamed shrilly, then it and the tree both disappeared.

Urlik nodded. 'You are as skilful as I heard you were, Merlin. And for an old man, still quick. But shall we give over this child's play?'

'It was not play, Urlik, as you well know.'

'No. But it was not a true test of strength. Dare you commit yourself to that?'

For a moment Merlin hesitated. 'It must finally come to that, must it not? You and what you stand for against all on our side.'

'Your side! What remains of your side but a small island whose king I already hold in the hollow of my hand?'

'A king you could not buy or bend to your will. That could be enough, Urlik.'

'Not if he dies. As he shall. And his army with him!'

'That remains to be seen. Still it might be as well to settle the matter here and now as have it drag on for years and continue to lay waste a whole world.'

'Then you will do it?'

Again Merlin hesitated. Then,

'Yes,' he said.

He handed Starflame back to Brian, took a deep breath as if gathering himself together, then made a circular motion with his right hand and the ring of light that had surrounded them faded and disappeared.

Urlik had settled himself in his iron throne as a warrior settles himself in the saddle before a charge. His green eyes glowed like those of a hungry wolf and when the ring of light faded they sought Merlin's and held them while Nimue at his side fixed her eyes on those of Blaise.

There was silence. And while, as before, nothing seemed to be happening, Brian sensed that forces beyond his comprehension were engaged in an unseen struggle; that all of Merlin's knowledge and will was locked in combat with Urlik as was that of Blaise with Nimue.

The room became colder with a deathly chill. The wind outside freshened and there was a clinking sound. Brian glanced up over Urlik's head and saw a length of chain blow in through the window behind the dais and then swing out again. A chain; the one Tertius had hung from Migbeg's sword on top of the keep. It was still there then. And though Tertius had said it was some kind of magic it had done them little good.

Brian brought his attention back to the silent struggle that was going on in the great hall. Merlin's face was strained and in spite of the chill in the air there were beads of sweat on his forehead and on Blaise's. Though Nimue was pale, she seemed composed while Urlik's expression and manner had not changed at all. His eyes still fixed on Merlin's, he looked like a wrestler, who while grappling with an antagonist of almost equal strength, knows that he still has reserves on which he can call.

Arthur stirred. 'Is there nothing you can do to help?' he whispered to Tertius. 'I spite of what Merlin said, I do not think they have their full strength back. In any case, they are sore beset.'

Tertius started. He had been intent but quiet since the silent struggle started like one caught on the fringe of a great battle and dazed by the noise, confusion and movements back and forth.

He nodded abruptly and raised his eyes to the window behind the dais. A tense look came over his face much like the one when he had tried to change the direction of the wind at Kerrec and, noting it, Lianor said, 'Easy. Remember the gentian.'

He glanced at her, forced a smile, then turned to the window again, making a complicated pass. There was a rumble of thunder in the distance, then another. Urlik's eyes went to him for a moment, then back to Merlin's. The veins in his forehead stood out as if he were putting forth all his strength. The sound of the wind grew louder and once more the end of the length of chain whipped in through the window, almost touching the back of Urlik's iron throne, then disappeared again. This time Nimue half turned to see what was happening and at once—as soon as she took her eyes from Blaise—she winced as if she had been struck a heavy blow and went reeling back almost to the wall behind her. Then, catching herself, she came forward to join the struggle again.

Tertius' eyes were still on the window, his face intent. Again thunder rumbled and now a flash of lightning lit up the great hall. It was still distant, but the thunder was almost continuous and growing louder. The veins on Urlik's forehead were dark and knotted now, his teeth showing as he strained at what he was doing. And Merlin staggered and almost fell. Like Nimue, he recovered but something seemed gone from him and slowly he was forced backward.

Tertius must have seen this out of the corner of his eye but he did not turn. His attention remained fixed on the window. The lightning flashed again and again, filling the hall with fitful light. Then as Urlik leaned forward, his strained look becoming one of triumph, there was a final deafening crash that shook the whole keep. The chain whipped in through the window again and this time the lightning was running down it. It leaped to the iron throne and the throne itself flamed with an eerie blue light. Urlik stiffened, then fell forward and lay still and Nimue, standing next to him, fell across him.

For a moment no one moved. Then, with cries of terror, the men-at-arms who stood about the walls dropped their weapons and fled from the hall. Merlin's knees gave way and if Brian and Arthur had not taken him by the arms and held him he would have fallen.

Straightening up, Merlin looked at Tertius.

'Did you do that?' he asked.

Tertius nodded.

'How? Urlik was said to be deathless.'

Tertius shook his head. 'The White Lady said he was not—even though nothing on earth or of the earth could kill him. So I called up a thunderstorm and brought down lightning to do it.'

'This was more of that untimely knowledge of yours?'

'I'm afraid so.'

'I said it might have some purpose that I was not aware of. It seems I was right.'

As Merlin looked at him thoughtfully there were distant shouts and the clash of arms and Arthur turned, listening.

'Our men have begun their assault. It may be that we can fight our way to the gatehouse, Brian, and lower the drawbridge for them.'

'Stay, Arthur,' said Merlin. 'Tertius will do it.'

'From here?' said Tertius. 'I'm not sure I can.'

'After what you did do?'

'There are things I can do and things I can't. I still have much to learn.'

Merlin continued to look at him, then nodded. Turning, he gestured. There was a rumbling crash as the drawbridge fell, a sound of battering as the gate was burst open and the shouts and clash of arms grew louder as Sir Owaine led his men into the castle.

'I think we should join them,' said Arthur.

'There is no need,' said Merlin. 'It is all over.'

'What about the rest of Urlik's forces?' asked Brian. 'He showed them to us in the magic mirror and said they were riding here.'

'Without Urlik they are nothing. They are far from home and now that they have no leader they will return there. Do you agree, Blaise?'

'Yes, Merlin,' said Blaise. 'As you said, it is over.'

He was leaning on Migbeg's arm, looking weary and more aged than ever.

'Though we stood side by side against Urlik and Nimue, we have not really talked yet,' said Merlin. 'How goes it with you, old friend?'

'Well enough, said Blaise. 'But despite that sight which I never expected to see,' and he indicated the bodies of Urlik and Nimue, 'I do not like this place. I feel as if I have been here far too long.'

'You have been,' said Merlin. 'The fighting outside must be over now also. If it is not, we will end it. In any case, we should go. But there is still much I do not know and much that should be talked about. So if it pleases you, Sire, I think we should gather at noon in your pavilion.'

'It pleases me well,' said Arthur.

*

The king's pavilion faced west and through the open doorway they could see the castle with Arthur's banner flying above the gatehouse and the sea beyond. They were all there: Arthur sitting on a campaign chair with Merlin and Blaise on either side of him and the Duke of Cornwall, Sir Owaine and Sir Constantine behind him. On stools facing them were Lianor, Brian, Tertius and those who had come with them; Migbeg, Giles, Long Hugh, Hob and Wat.

The tale of all that had happened had been told, interrupted by the coming and going of scouts who confirmed Merlin's statement about the Mongols. For on Arthur's orders all those who had not been slain in the taking of the castle had been released to spread word of the death of Urlik and at last report his armies were not merely withdrawing but fleeing eastward, harried and pursued by all those whose lands they had conquered.

'Then it is as you said, Merlin, all over,' said Arthur.

'This much at least—this threat which was a great one,' said Merlin gravely.

'There will be others?'

'Nothing is won forever as nothing can be built that will last forever. If it were otherwise, what would there be for the young to do?'

'And what of those of us who are no longer young? What is there for us?'

'If we are fortunate, moments of peace—time to remember that which we have done and found good.'

'What I will remember,' said the king, 'is not what I did but what others did; all of you gathered here before me. For all of you played a part in this great adventure. And none of you shall lack proof of my love and gratitude.'

'I cannot speak for the others, Sire,' said Brian, 'but if you are thinking of rewards, mine lies in this moment; in the knowledge that you and Britain are safe and that Merlin and Blaise are with us again to keep you both so.'

'I expected no less of you, Brian,' said the king. 'Nor of the rest of you.' For they had all nodded their agreement. 'But you must not deny me the pleasure of requiting you in whatever way seems most appropriate. In some cases,' and he looked at the outlaws, 'that will be easy. In some,' and he looked at Lianor and Brian, Migbeg and Giles, 'it will be less easy but I am sure I will think of something I can do for you. However you, Tertius, are a puzzle. For though, as I said, all of you played a part in this, in the end it was you who did what none thought could be done by destroying Urlik. How can I—or anyone—repay you for that?'

'And what have you done to repay me for all that I have done for you since the day you were born, Sire?' asked Merlin.

'I do not know that I have done anything, but I have loved you, honoured you and trusted you.'

'That was my reward. And in time it will be his. But not yet. For,' turning to Tertius, 'did you not say you still had much to learn?'

'Yes, Merlin.'

'Good. I am glad to see that what you know and what you have accomplished has not given you too good an opinion of yourself.'

'Which,' said Blaise with a faint smile, 'is more than can be said of you, Merlin, when you were his age and my disciple.'